Other Mystery Novels by Cornell Woolrich

I Married a Dead Man

Cornell Woolrich

The Best Mysteries of All Time

THE BEST MYSTERIES OF ALL TIME

I MARRIED A DEAD MAN

ImPress is an imprint of The Reader's Digest Association, Inc.,
Bedford Road, Pleasantville, New York 10570.

Library of Congress Cataloging-in-Publication Data

Woolrich, Cornell, 1903–1968.
  I married a dead man / by Cornell Woolrich.
    p. cm.—(The best mysteries of all time)
  ISBN 0-7621-8890-1
  1. Impostors and imposture—Fiction. 2. Pregnant women—Fiction.
  3. Extortion—Fiction. I. Title. II. Series.
PS3515.O6455I23 2003
814'.52—dc21   2003001993

PRINTED IN THE UNITED STATES OF AMERICA

I Married a Dead Man

THE summer nights are so pleasant in Caulfield. They smell of heliotrope and jasmine, honeysuckle and clover. The stars are warm and friendly here, not cold and distant, as where I came from; they seem to hang lower over us, be closer to us. The breeze that stirs the curtains at the open windows is soft and gentle as a baby's kiss. And on it, if you listen, you can hear the rustling sound of the leafy trees turning over and going back to sleep again. The lamplight from within the houses falls upon the lawns outside and copperplates them in long swaths. There's the hush, the stillness of perfect peace and security. Oh yes, the summer nights are pleasant in Caulfield.

But not for us.

The winter nights are too. The nights of fall, the nights of spring. Not for us, not for us.

The house we live in is so pleasant in Caulfield. The blue-green tint of its lawn that always seems so freshly watered no matter what the time of day. The sparkling, aerated pinwheels of the sprinklers always turning, steadily turning; if you look at them closely enough, they form rainbows before your eyes. The clean, sharp curve of the driveway. The dazzling whiteness of the porch supports in the sun. Indoors, the curving white symmetry of the banister, as gracious as the dark and glossy stair it accompanies down from above. The satin finish of the rich old floors, bearing a telltale scent of wax and of lemon oil if you stop to sniff. The lushness of pile carpeting. In almost every room, some favorite chair waiting to greet you like an old friend when you come back to spend a little time with it. People who come and see it say, "What more can there be? This is a home, as a home should be." Yes, the house we live in is so pleasant in Caulfield.

But not for us.

Our little boy, our Hugh, his and mine, it's such a joy to watch him growing up in Caulfield. In the house that will someday be his, in the town that will someday be his. To watch him take the first tottering steps that mean, now he can walk. To catch and cherish each newly minted word that fumblingly issues from his lips—that means, now he's added another, now he can talk.

But even that is not for us, somehow. Even that seems thefted, stolen, in some vague way I cannot say. Something we're not entitled to, something that isn't rightfully ours.

I love him so. It's Bill I mean now, the man. And he loves me. I know I do, I know he does, I cannot doubt it. And yet I know just as surely that on some day to come, maybe this year, maybe next, suddenly he'll pack his things and go away and leave me. Though he won't want to. Though he'll love me still, as much as he does on the day that I say this.

Or if he doesn't, it will be I who will. I'll take up my valise and walk out through the door, never to come back. Though I won't want to. Though I'll love him still, as much as I do on the day that I say this. I'll leave my house behind. I'll leave my baby behind, in the house that will someday be his, and I'll leave my heart behind, with the man it belongs to (how could I take it with me?), but I'll go and I'll never come back.

We've fought this thing. How bitterly we've fought it, in every way that we know how. In every way there is. We've driven it away, a thousand times we've driven it away, and it comes back again in a look, a word, a thought. It's there.

No good for me to say to him, "You didn't do it. You've told me so once. Once was enough. No need to repeat it now again, this late. I *know* you didn't. Oh, my darling, my Bill, you don't lie. You don't lie, in money, or in honor, or in love—"

(But this isn't money, or honor, or love. This is a thing apart. This is murder.)

No good, when I don't believe him. At the moment that he speaks, I may. But a moment later, or an hour, or a day or week, again I don't. No good, for we don't live just within a single moment, we can't. The other moments come, the hours, weeks, and, oh God, the years.

For each time, as he speaks, I know it wasn't I. That's all I know. So well, too well, I know. And that leaves only—

And each time, as I speak, perhaps he knows that it wasn't he (but I cannot know that, I cannot; there is no way for him to reach me). So well he knows, so well. And that leaves only—

No good, no good at all.

One night six months ago I dropped upon my knees before him, with the boy there between us. Upon my bended knees. I put my hand on the little boy's head, and I swore it to him then and there. Speaking low, so the child wouldn't understand.

"By my child. Bill, I swear to you on the head of my child that I didn't. Oh Bill, I didn't do it—"

He raised me up, and held me in his arms, and pressed me to him.

"I know you didn't. I know. What more can I say? In what other way can I tell you? Here, lie against my heart, Patrice. Perhaps that can tell you better than I— Listen to it. Can't you tell that it believes you?"

And for a moment it does, that one moment of our love. But then the other moment comes, that one that always comes after. And he has already thought, "But I know it wasn't I. I know so well it wasn't I. And that leaves only—"

And even while his arms go tighter than ever about me, and his lips kiss the wetness from my eyes, he already doesn't again. He already doesn't.

There's no way out. We're caught, we're trapped. The circle viciously completes itself each time, and we're on the inside, can't break through. For if he's innocent, then it has to be me. And if I am, it has to be he. But I *know* I'm innocent. (Yet he may know he is too.) There's no way out.

Or, tired with trying to drive it away, we've rushed toward it with desperate abandon, tried to embrace it, to be done with it once and for all in that way.

One time, unable to endure its long-drawn, unseen, ghostly vigil over our shoulders any longer, he suddenly flung himself out of the chair he'd been in, though nothing had been said between us for an hour past. Flung the book he hadn't been reading, only pretending to, far from him like a brickbat. Flung himself up as wildly as though he were going to rush forward to grapple with something he saw there before him. And my heart flung itself wildly up with him.

He surged to the far end of the room and stopped there—at bay. And made a fist, and raised his arm, and swung it with a thundering crash against the door, so that only the panel's thickness kept it from shattering. Then turned in his helpless defiance and cried out, "I don't care! It doesn't matter! Do you hear me? It doesn't matter! People have done it before. Lots of times. And lived out their happiness afterward. Why shouldn't we? He was no good. It was what he deserved. He wasn't worth a second thought. The whole world said so then, and they'd still say so now. He isn't worth a single minute of this hell we've gone through."

And then he poured a drink for each of us, lavish, reckless, and came back toward me with them. And I, understanding, agreeing, one with him, rose and went to meet him halfway.

"Here, take this. Drink on it. Drown it. Drown it until it's gone. One of us *did* do it. It doesn't matter. It's done with. Now let's get on with living." And striking himself on the chest, "All right, *I* did it. There. I was the one. Now it's settled. Now it's over at last."

And then suddenly our eyes looked deep into one another's, our glasses faltered in midair, went down, and it was back again.

"But you don't believe that," I whispered, dismayed.

"And you do," he breathed, stricken.

Oh, it's everything, it's everywhere.

We've gone away, and it's where we go. It's in the blue depths of Lake Louise and high up in the fleecy cloud formations above Biscayne Bay. It rolls restlessly in with the surf at Santa Barbara and lurks amid the coral rocks of Bermuda, a darker flower than the rest.

We've come back, and it's where we've come back to.

It's between the printed lines on the pages of the books we read. But it peers forth dark, and they fade off to illegibility. "Is he thinking of it now, as I read? As I am? I will not look up at him, I will keep my eyes to this, but—is he thinking of it now?"

It's the hand that holds out its coffee cup across the breakfast table in the mornings, to have the urn tipped over it. Bloody red for a moment in fancy, then back again to pale as it should be. Or maybe, to the other, it's that other hand opposite one that does the tipping of the urn; depending upon which side of the table the beholder is sitting.

I saw his eyes rest on my hand one day, and I knew what he was thinking at that instant. Because I had looked at his hand much the same way on a previous day, and I had been thinking then what he was thinking now.

I saw him close his eyes briefly, to efface the sickly illusion; and I closed mine to dispel the knowledge of it that his had conveyed to me. Then we both opened them, and smiled at one another, to tell one another nothing had happened just then.

It's in the pictures that we see on the theater screen. "Let's get out of here. I'm—tired of it. Aren't you?" (Somebody is going to kill somebody, up there, soon, and he knows it's coming.) But even though we do get up and leave, it's already too late, because he knows why we're leaving, and I know too. And even if I didn't know until then, this—the very fact of our leaving—has told me.

So the precaution is wasted after all. *It's* back in our minds again.

Still, it's wiser to go than to stay.

I remember one night it came too quickly, more suddenly than we could have foretold; there was less warning given. We were not able to get all the way out in time. We were still only making our way up the aisle, our backs to the screen, when suddenly a shot rang out, and then a voice groaned in accusation, "You've—you've killed me."

It seemed to me it was *his* voice, and that he was speaking to us, to one of us. It seemed to me, in that moment, that every head in the audience turned, to look our way, to stare at us, with that detached curiosity of a great crowd when someone has been pointed out to them.

My legs for a moment seemed to refuse to carry me any further. I floundered there for a minute as though I were going to fall down helpless upon the carpeted aisle. I turned to look at him, and I saw, unmistakably, that his head had cringed for a moment, was down defensively between his shoulders. And he always carried it so straight and erect. A moment later it *was* straight again, but just for that instant it hadn't been, it had been hunched.

Then, as though sensing that I needed him just then, because, perhaps, he needed me, he put his arm around my waist and helped me the rest of the way up the aisle that way, steadying me, promising me support rather than actually giving it to me.

In the lobby, both our faces were like chalk. We didn't look at one another; it was the mirrors on the side told us that.

We never drink. We know enough not to. I think we sense that, rather than close the door on awareness, that would only open it all the wider and let full horror in. But that particular night, I remember, as we came out, he said, "Do you want something?"

He didn't say a drink, just "something." But I understood what that "something" meant. "Yes," I shuddered quietly.

We didn't even wait until we got home; it would have taken us too long. We went in to a place next door to the theater and stood up to the bar for a moment, the two of us alike, and gulped down something on the run. In three minutes we were out of there again. Then we got in the car and drove home. And we never said a word the whole way.

It's in the very kiss we give each other. Somehow we trap it right between our lips, each time. (Did I kiss him too strongly? Will he think by that I forgave him, again, just then? Did I kiss him too weakly? Will he think by that I was thinking of it, again, just then?)

It's everywhere, it's all the time, it's *us*.

I don't know what the game was. I only know its name; they call it life.

I'm not sure how it should be played. No one ever told me. No one ever tells anybody. I only know we must have played it wrong. We broke some rule or other along the way and never knew it at the time.

I don't know what the stakes are. I only know we've forfeited them; they're not for us.

We've lost. That's all I know. We've lost, we've lost.

THE door was closed. It had a look of pitiless finality about it, as though it would always be closed like this from now on. As though nothing in the world could ever make it open again. Doors can express things. This one did. It was inert; it was life-less; it didn't lead anywhere. It was not the beginning of anything, as a door should be. It was the ending of something.

Above the push button there was a small oblong rack of metal affixed to the woodwork, intended to frame a name card. It was empty. The card was gone.

The girl was standing still in front of the door. Perfectly still. The way you stand when you've been standing for a long time; so long, you've forgotten about moving, have grown used to not moving. Her finger was to the push button, but it wasn't pushing anymore. No pressure was being exerted; no sound came from the battery behind the doorframe. It was as though she had been holding it that way so long, she had forgotten to take that, too, away.

She was about nineteen. A dreary, hopeless nineteen, not a bright, shiny one. Her features were small and well turned, but there was something too pinched about her face, too wan about her coloring, too thin about her cheeks. Beauty was there, implicit, ready to reclaim her face if it was given the chance, but something had beaten it back, was keeping it hovering at a distance, unable to alight in its intended realization.

Her hair was hazel-colored, and limp and listless, as though no great heed had been paid to it for some time past. The heels of her shoes were a little run-down. A puckered darn in the heel of her stocking peered just over the top of one. Her clothing was functional, as though it were worn for the sake of covering, and not for the sake of fashion or even of appeal. She was a good height for a girl, about five six or seven. But she was too thin, except in one place.

Her head was down a little, as though she were tired of carrying it up straight. Or as though invisible blows had lowered it, one by one.

She moved at last. At long last. Her hand dropped from the push button, as if of its own weight. It fell to her side, hung there, forlorn. One foot turned, as if to go away. There was a wait. Then the other turned too. Her back was to the door now. The door that wouldn't open. The door that was an epitaph, the door that was finality.

She took a slow step away. Then another. Her head was down

now more than ever. She moved slowly away from there and left the door behind. Her shadow was the last part of her to go. It trailed slowly after her, upright against the wall. Its head was down a little too; it too was too thin; it too was unwanted. It stayed on a moment, after she herself was already gone. Then it slipped off the wall after her, and *it* was gone too.

Nothing was left there but the door. That remained silent, obdurate, closed.

IN THE telephone booth she was motionless again. As motionless as before. A telephone pay station, the door left shunted back in order to obtain air enough to breathe. When you are in one for more than just a few moments, they become stifling. And she had been in this one for more than just a few moments.

She was like a doll propped upright in its gift box, and with one side of the box left off, to allow the contents to be seen. A worn doll. A leftover, marked-down doll, with no bright ribbons or tissue wrappings. A doll with no donor and no recipient. A doll no one bothered to claim.

She was silent there, though this was meant to be a place for talking. She was waiting to hear something, something that never came. She was holding the receiver pointed toward her ear, and it must have started out by being close to it, at right angles to it, as receivers should be. But that was a long time before. With the passage of long, disappointing minutes it had drooped lower and lower, until now it was all the way down at her shoulder, clinging there wilted, defeated, like some sort of ugly, black, hard-rubber orchid worn for corsage.

The anonymous silence became a voice at last. But not the one she wanted, not the one she was waiting for.

"I am sorry, but I have already told you. There is no use waiting on the line. That number has been discontinued, and there is no further information I can give you."

Her hand dropped off her shoulder, carrying the receiver with it, and fell into her lap, dead. As if to match something else within her that was dead, by the final way it fell and stirred no more.

But life won't grant a decent dignity even to its epitaphs, sometimes.

"May I have my nickel back?" she whispered. "*Please.* I didn't get my party, and it's—it's the last one I've got."

3

SHE climbed the rooming-house stairs like a puppet dangling from slack strings. A light bracketed against the wall, drooping upside down like a withered tulip in its bell-shaped shade of scalloped glass, cast a smoky yellow glow. A carpet strip ground to the semblance of decayed vegetable matter, all pattern, all color, long erased, adhered to the middle of the stairs, like a form of pollen or fungus encrustation. The odor matched the visual imagery. She climbed three flights of them and then turned off toward the back.

She stopped at the last door there was and took out a long-shanked iron key. Then she looked down at the bottom of the door. There was a triangle of white down by her foot, protruding from under the seam. It expanded into an envelope as the door swept back above it.

She reached into the darkness and traced her hand along the wall beside the door, and a light went on. It had very little shine. It had very little to shine on.

She closed the door, and then she picked up the envelope. It had been lying on its face. She turned it over. Her hand shook a little. Her heart did too.

It had on it, in hasty, heedless pencil, only this:

Helen Georgesson

No Miss, no Mrs., no other salutation whatever.

She seemed to come alive more fully. Some of the blank hopelessness left her eyes. Some of the pinched strain left her face. She grasped the envelope tight, until it pleated a little in her hold. She moved more briskly than she had until now. She took it over with her to the middle of the room, beside the bed, where the light shone more fully.

She stood still there and looked at it again, as though she were a little afraid of it. There was a sort of burning eagerness in her face; not joyous, but rather of desperate urgency.

She ripped hastily at the flap of it, with upward swoops of her hand, as though she were taking long stitches in it with invisible needle and thread.

Her hand plunged in, to pull out what it said, to read what it told her. For envelopes carry words that tell you things; that's what envelopes are for.

Her hand came out again empty, frustrated. She turned the envelope over and shook it out, to free what it must hold, what must have stubbornly resisted her fingers the first time.

No words came, no writing.

Two things fell out, onto the bed. Only two things.

One was a five-dollar bill. Just an impersonal, anonymous five-dollar bill, with Lincoln's picture on it. And over to the side of that, the neat little cachet they all bear, in small-size capitals: "This certificate is legal tender for all debts public and private." For all debts, public and *private*. How could the engraver guess that that might break somebody's heart, someday, somewhere?

And the second thing was a strip of railroad tickets, running consecutively from starting point to terminus, as railroad tickets do. Each coupon to be detached progressively en route. The first coupon was inscribed "New York"—here, where she was now. And the last was inscribed "San Francisco," where she'd come from, a hundred years ago—last spring.

There was no return ticket. It was for a one-way trip. There and—to stay.

So the envelope *had* spoken to her after all, though it had no words in it. Five dollars legal tender, for *all* debts, public and private. San Francisco—and no return.

The envelope plummeted to the floor.

She couldn't seem to understand for a long time. It was as though she'd never seen a five-dollar bill before. It was as though she'd never seen an accordion-pleated strip of railroad tickets like that before. She kept staring down at them.

Then she started to shake a little. At first without sound. Her face kept twitching intermittently, up alongside the eyes and down around the corners of the mouth, as if her expression were struggling to burst forth into some kind of fulminating emotion. For a moment or two it seemed that when it did, it would be weeping. But it wasn't.

It was laughter.

Her eyes wreathed into oblique slits, and her lips slashed back, and harsh broken sounds came through. Like rusty laughter. Like laughter left in the rain too long, that has got all mildewed and spoiled.

She was still laughing when she brought out the battered valise, and placed it atop the bed, and threw the lid back. She was still laughing when she'd filled it and closed it again.

She never seemed to get through laughing. Her laughter never stopped. As at some long-drawn joke that goes on and on and is never done with in its telling.

But laughter should be merry, vibrant, and alive.

This wasn't.

THE train had already ticked off fifteen minutes' solid, steady headway, and she hadn't yet found a seat. The seats were full with holiday crowds, and the aisles were full, and the very vestibules were full; she'd never seen a train like this before. She'd been too far behind at the dammed-up barrier, and too slow and awkward with her cumbersome valise, and too late getting on. Her ticket only allowed her to get aboard; it gave her no priority on any place to sit.

Flagging, wilting, exhausted, she struggled down car aisle after car aisle, walking backward against the train pull, eddying, teetering from side to side, leaden valise pulling her down.

They were all packed with standees, and this was the last one now. No more cars after this. She'd been through them all. No one offered her a seat. This was a through train, no stops for whole states at a time, and an act of courtesy now would have come too high. This was no trolley or bus with a few moments' running time. Once you were gallant and stood, you stood for hundreds and hundreds of miles.

She stopped at last, and stayed where she'd stopped, for sheer inability to turn and go back again to where she'd come from. No use going any further. She could see to the end of the car, and there weren't any left.

She let her valise down parallel to the aisle and tried to seat herself upon its upturned edge, as she saw so many others doing. But she floundered badly for a moment, out of her own top-heaviness, and almost tumbled in lowering herself. Then when she'd succeeded, she let her head settle back against the sideward edge of the seat she was adjacent to, and stayed that way. Too tired to know, too tired to care, too tired even to close her eyes.

What makes you stop, when you have stopped, just where you have stopped? What is it, what? Is it something, or is it nothing? Why not a yard short, why not a yard more? Why just there where you are, and nowhere else?

Some say, It's just blind chance, and if you hadn't stopped there, you would have stopped at the next place. Your story would have been different then. You weave your own story as you go along.

But others say, You could not have stopped anyplace else but this even if you had wanted to. It was decreed, it was ordered, you were meant to stop at this spot and no other. Your story is there waiting for you; it has been waiting for you there a hundred years, long before you were born, and you cannot change a comma of it.

Everything you do, you have to do. You are the twig, and the water you float on swept you here. You are the leaf, and the breeze you were borne on blew you here. This is your story, and you cannot escape it; you are only the player, not the stage manager. Or so some say.

On the floor before her downcast eyes, just over the rim of the seat arm, she could see two pairs of shoes uptilted, side by side. On the inside, toward the window, a diminutive pair of pumps, pert, saucy, without backs, without sides, without toes, in fact with scarcely anything but dagger-like heels and a couple of straps. And on the outside, the nearer side to her, a pair of man's brogues, looking by comparison squat, bulky, and tremendously heavy. These hung one above the other, from legs coupled at the knee.

She did not see their faces, and she did not want to. She did not want to see anyone's face. She did not want to see anything.

Nothing happened for a moment. Then one of the pumps edged slyly over toward one of the brogues, nudged gently into it, as if in a deft little effort to communicate something. The brogue remained oblivious; it didn't get the message. It got the feeling, but not the intent. A large hand came down and scratched tentatively at the sock just above the brogue, then went up again.

The pump, as if impatient at such obtuseness, repeated the effort. Only this time it delivered a good sharp dig, with a bite to it, and on the unprotected ankle, above the armor-like brogue.

That got results. A newspaper rattled somewhere above, as if it had been lowered out of the way, to see what all this unpleasant nipping was about.

A whispered remark was voiced above, spoken too low to be distinguishable by any but the ear for which it was intended.

An interrogative grunt, in masculine timbre, answered it.

Both brogues came down even on the floor as the legs above uncoupled. Then they swiveled slightly toward the aisle, as if their owner had turned his upper body to glance that way.

The girl on the valise closed her eyes wearily, to avoid the gaze that she knew must be on her.

When she opened them again, the brogues had come out through the seat gap, and the wearer was standing full height in the aisle, on the other side of her. A good height too, a six-foot height.

"Take my seat, miss," he invited. "Go ahead, take my place for a while."

She tried to demur with a faint smile and a halfhearted shake of the head. But the velour back looked awfully good.

The girl who had remained in it added her insistence to his. "Go ahead, honey, take it," she urged. "He wants you to. We want you to. You can't stay out there like that, where you are."

The velour back looked awfully good. She couldn't take her eyes off it. But she was almost too tired to stand up and effect the change. He had to reach down and take her by the arm and help her rise from the valise and shift over.

Her eyes closed again for a moment, in ineffable bliss, as she sank back.

"There you are," he said heartily. "Isn't that better?"

And the girl beside her, her new seatmate, said, "Why, you *are* tired. I never saw anyone so all-in."

She smiled her thanks, and still tried to protest a little, though the act had already been completed, but they both overrode her remonstrances.

She looked at the two of them. Now she at least wanted to see their two faces, if no others, though only a few moments ago she hadn't wanted to see any faces, anywhere, ever again. But kindness is a form of restorative.

They were both young. Well, she was too. But they were both happy, gay, basking in the world's blessings; that was the difference between them and her. It stood out all over them. There was some sort of gilded incandescence alight within both of them alike, something that was more than mere good spirits, more than mere good fortune, and for the first few moments she couldn't tell what it was. Then in no time at all, their eyes, and every turn of their heads, and every move they made, gave it away: they were supremely, brimmingly in love with one another. It glowed out all over them, almost like phosphorus.

Young love. New untarnished love. That first love that comes just once to everyone and never comes back again.

But, conversationally, it expressed itself inversely, at least on her part if not his; almost every remark she addressed to him was a friendly insult, a gentle slur, an amiable depreciation. Not so much as a word of tenderness, or even ordinary human consideration, did she seem to have for him. Though her eyes belied her. And he understood. He had that smile for all her outrageous insolences, that worshipped, that adored, that understood so well.

"Well, go on," she said with a peremptory flick of her hand. "Don't stand there like a dope, breathing down the backs of our necks. Go and find something to do."

"Oh, pardon me," he said, and pretended to turn the back of his collar up, as if frozen out. He looked vaguely up and down the aisle. "Guess I'll go out on the platform and smoke a cigarette."

"Smoke two," she said airily. "See if I care."

He turned and began to pick his way down the thronged aisle.

"That was nice of him," the newcomer said appreciatively, glancing after him.

"Oh, he's tolerable," her companion said. "He has his good points." She gave a shrug. But her eyes made a liar out of her.

She glanced around to make sure he'd gone out of earshot. Then she leaned slightly toward the other, dropped her voice confidentially. "I could tell right away," she said. "That's why I made him get up. About you, I mean."

The girl who'd been on the valise dropped her eyes for an instant, confused, deprecating. She didn't say anything.

"I am too. You're not the only one," her companion rushed on, with just a trace of vainglory, as if she couldn't wait to tell it quickly enough.

The girl said, "Oh." She didn't know what else to say. It sounded flat, superficial; the way you say "Is that so?" or "You don't say?" She tried to force a smile of sympathetic interest, but she wasn't very good at it. Out of practice at smiling, maybe.

"Seven months," the other added gratuitously.

The girl could feel her eyes on her, as though she expected some return in kind to be made, if only for the record.

"Eight," she said, half audibly. She didn't want to, but she did.

"Wonderful," was her companion's praise for this arithmetical information. "Marvelous." As though there were some sort of a caste system involved in this, and she unexpectedly found herself speaking to one of the upper brackets of nobility: a duchess or a marquise, who outranked her by thirty days. And all around them, snobbishly ignored, the commonality of the female gender.

"Wonderful, marvelous," echoed the girl inwardly, and her heart gave a frightened, unheard sob.

"And your husband?" the other rushed on. "You going to meet him?"

"No," the girl said, looking steadily at the green velour of the seat-back in front of them. "No."

"Oh. D'dyou leave him back in New York?"

"No," the girl said. "No." She seemed to see it written on the seat-back in transitory lettering that faded again as soon as it was once read. "I've lost him."

"Oh, I'm sor—" Her vivacious companion seemed to know grief for the first time, other than just grief over a broken doll or a schoolgirl crush betrayed. It was like a new experience passing over her radiant face. And it was, even now, bound to be someone else's grief, not her own; that was the impression you had. That she'd never had any grief of her own, had none now, and never would have. One of those star-blessed rarities, glittering its way through the world's dark vale.

She bit off the rest of the ejaculation of sympathy, gnawed at her upper lip, reached out impulsively, and placed her hand upon her companion's for a moment, then withdrew it again.

Then, tactfully, they didn't speak anymore about such things. Such basic things as birth and death, that can give such joy and can give such pain.

She had corn-gold hair, this sun-kissed being. She wore it in a hazy aureole that fluffed out all over her head. She had freckles that were like little flecks of gold paint, spattered from some careless painter's brush all over her apricot cheeks, with a saddle across the bridge of her tiny, pert nose. It was her mouth that was the beautiful part of her. And if the rest of her face was not quite up to its matchless beauty, that mouth alone was sufficient to make her lovely-looking, unaided, drawing all notice to itself as it did. Just as a single light is enough to make a plain room bright; you don't have to have a whole chandelier. When it smiled, everything else smiled with it. Her nose crinkled, and her eyebrows arched, and her eyes creased, and dimples showed up where there hadn't been any a minute before. She looked as though she smiled a lot. She looked as though she had a lot to smile about.

She continually toyed with a wedding band on her third finger. Caressed it, so to speak, fondled it. She was probably unconscious of doing so by this time; it must have become a fixed habit by now. But originally, months ago, when it was first there, when it was new there, she must have taken such a fierce pride in it that she'd felt the need for continually displaying it to all the world— as if to say, "Look at *me!* Look what I've got!"—must have held such an affection for it that she couldn't keep her hands off it for very long. And now, though pride and affection were in nowise less, this had formed itself into a winning little habit that persisted. No matter what move her hands made, no matter what gesture they expressed, it always managed to come uppermost, to be foremost in the beholder's eye.

It had a row of diamonds and then a sapphire at each end for a stop. She caught her new seatmate's glance resting upon it, so then she turned it around her way a little more, so she could see it all the better, gave it a pert little brush-off with her fingers, as if to dispel the last, lingering, hypothetical grain of dust. A brush-off that pretended she didn't care anymore about it just then. Just as her attitude toward him pretended she didn't care anything about him either. A brush-off that lied like the very devil.

They were both chatting away absorbedly, as newfound friends do, by the time he reappeared some ten minutes later. He came up to them acting secretive and mysterious in a rather conspicu-ous way. He looked cautiously left and right first, as if bearing tid-ings of highest secrecy. Then screened the side of his mouth with the edge of one hand. Then leaned down and whispered, "Pat, one of the porters just tipped me off. They're going to open up the dining car in a couple of minutes. Special, inside, advance information. You know what that'll mean in this mob. I think we better start moving up that way if we want to get in under the rope on the first shift. There'll be a stampede under way as soon as word gets around."

She jumped to her feet with alacrity.

He immediately soft-pedaled her with the flats of both hands, in comic intensity. "Sh! Don't give it away! What are you trying to do? Act indifferent. Act as if you weren't going anywhere in particular, were just getting up to stretch your legs."

She smothered an impish chuckle. "When I'm going to the dining car, I just *can't* act as if I weren't going anywhere in par-ticular. It stands out all over me. You're lucky if you hold me down to a twenty-yard dash." But to oblige his ideas of Machi-avellian duplicity, she exaggeratedly arched her feet and tiptoed out into the aisle, as though the amount of noise she made had any relation to what they were trying to do.

In passing, she pulled persuasively at the sleeve of the girl beside her. "Come on. You're coming with us, aren't you?" she whispered conspiratorially.

"What about the seats? We'll lose them, won't we?"

"Not if we put our baggage on them. Here, like this." She raised the other girl's valise, which had been standing there in the aisle until now, and between them they planked it lengthwise across the seat, effectively blocking it.

The girl was on her feet now, dislodged by the valise, but she still hung back, hesitant about going with them.

The young wife seemed to understand; she was quick that way. She sent him on ahead, out of earshot, to break trail for them. Then turned to her recent seatmate in tactful reassurance. "Don't worry about—anything; *he*'ll look after everything." And then, making confidantes of the two of them about this, to minimize the other's embarrassment, she promised her, "I'll see that he does. That's what they're for, anyway."

The girl tried to falter an insincere denial that only proved the surmise had been right. "No, it isn't that— I don't like to—"

But her new friend had already taken her acceptance for an accomplished fact, had no more time to waste on it. "Hurry up, we'll lose him," she urged. "They're closing in again behind him."

She urged her forward ahead of herself, a friendly hand lightly placed just over her outside hip.

"You can't neglect yourself now, of all times," she cautioned her in an undertone. "I *know*. They told me that myself."

The pioneering husband, meanwhile, was cutting a wide swath for them down the center of the clogged aisle, causing people to lean acutely in over the seats to give clearance. And yet with never a resentful look. He seemed to have that way about him—genial but firm.

"It's useful to have a husband who used to be on the football team," his bride commented complacently. "He can run your interference for you. Just look at the width of that back, would you?"

When they had overtaken him, she complained petulantly, "Wait for me, can't you? I have two to feed."

"So have I," was the totally unchivalrous remark over his shoulder. "And they're both me."

They were, by dint of his foresight, the first ones in the dining car, which was inundated within moments after the doors had been thrown open. They secured a choice table for three, diagonal to a window. The unlucky ones had to wait on line in the aisle outside, the door inhospitably closed in their faces.

"Just so we won't sit down to the table still not knowing each other's names," the young wife said, cheerfully unfolding her napkin, "he's Hazzard, Hugh, and I'm Hazzard, Patrice." Her dimples showed up in depreciation. "Funny name, isn't it?"

"Be more respectful," her young spouse growled, without lifting his forehead from the bill of fare. "I'm just trying you out for it. I haven't decided yet whether I'll let you keep it or not."

"It's mine now," was the feminine logic he got. "I haven't decided whether I'll let *you* keep it or not."

"What's your name?" she asked their guest.

"Georgesson," the girl said. "Helen Georgesson."

She smiled hesitantly at the two of them. Gave him the outside edge of her smile, gave her the center of it. It wasn't a very broad smile, but it had depth and gratitude, the little there was of it.

"You've both been awfully friendly to me," she said.

She looked down at the menu card she held spread between her hands so they wouldn't detect the flicker of emotion that made her lips tremble for a moment.

"It must be an awful lot of fun to be—you," she murmured wistfully.

By the time the overhead lights in their car had been put out,
around ten, so that those who wanted to sleep could do so, they
were already old and fast friends. They were already "Patrice"
and "Helen" to one another; this, as might have been surmised,
at Patrice's instigation. Friendship blooms quickly in the hot-
house atmosphere of travel; within the space of hours, sometimes, it's already full-blown. Then just as suddenly is snapped
off short, by the inevitable separation of the travelers. It seldom
if ever survives that separation for long. That is why, on ships
and trains, people have fewer reticences with one another; they
exchange confidences more quickly, tell all about themselves.
They will never have to see these same people again and worry

about what opinion they may have formed, whether good or bad.

The small, shaded, individual sidelights provided for each seat, that could be turned on or off at will, were still on for the most part, but the car was restfully dimmer and quieter, some of its occupants already dozing. Patrice's husband was in an inert, hat-shrouded state on the valise that again stood alongside his original seat, his crossed legs precariously slung upward to the top of the seat ahead. However, he seemed comfortable enough, judging by the sonorous sounds that escaped from inside his hat now and then. He had dropped out of their conversation fully an hour before, and, an unkind commentary this on the importance of men to women's conversations, to all appearances hadn't even been missed.

Patrice was acting the part of a lookout, her eyes watchfully and jealously fastened on a certain door, far down the aisle behind them, in the dim distance. To do this, she was kneeling erect on the seat, in reverse, staring vigilantly over the back of it. This somewhat unconventional position, however, did nothing whatever to inhibit her conversational flow, which proceeded as freely and blithely as ever. Only, owing to her elevated stance, the next seat back now shared the benefit of most of it, along with her own. Fortunately, however, its occupants were disqualified from any great amount of interest in it by two facts: they were both men, and they were both asleep.

A ripple of reflected light suddenly ran down the sleek chromium of the door that had her attention.

"She just came out," she hissed with an explosive sibilance, and executed an agitated series of twists, turns, and drops on the seat, as though this were something vital that had to be acted upon immediately. "Hurry up! *Now!* Now's our chance. Get a move on.

Before somebody else gets there ahead of us. There's a fat woman three seats down been taking her things out little by little. If she ever gets in first, we're sunk!" Carried away by her own excitement (and everything in life, to her, seemed to be deliciously, titillatingly exciting), she even went so far as to give her seatmate a little push and urge her: "Run! Hold the door for us. Maybe if she sees you there already, she'll change her mind."

She prodded her relaxed spouse cruelly and heartlessly in a great many places at once, to bring him back to awareness.

"Quick! Hugh! The overnight case! We'll lose our chance. Up there, stupid. Up there on the rack—"

"All right, take it easy," the somnolent Hugh grunted, eyes still completely buried under his obliterating hat brim. "Talk, talk, talk. Yattatta, yattatta, yattatta. Woman is born to exercise her jaw."

"Man is born to get a poke on his, if he doesn't get a move on."

He finally pushed his hat back out of the way. "What do you want from me now? You got it down yourself."

"Well, get your big legs out of the way and let us by! You're blocking the way—"

He executed a sort of drawbridge maneuver, folding his legs back to himself, hugging them, then stretching them out again after the passage had been accomplished.

"Where y'going in such a hurry?" he asked innocently.

"Now, isn't that stupid?" commented Patrice to her companion.

The two of them went almost running down the aisle, without bothering to enlighten him further.

"He takes a thirty-six sleeve, and it doesn't do me a bit of good in an emergency," she complained en route, swinging the kit.

He had turned his head to watch them curiously, and in

perfectly sincere incomprehension. Then he went, "Oh." Understanding their destination now, if not the turmoil attendant on it. Then he pulled his hat down to his nose again, to resume his fractured slumbers where they had been broken off by this feminine logistical upheaval.

Patrice had closed the chromium door after the two of them, meanwhile, and given its inside lock control a little twist of defiant exclusion. Then she let out a deep breath. "There. We're in. And possession is nine-tenths of the law. I'm going to take as long as I want," she announced determinedly, setting down the overnight case and unlatching its lid. "If anybody else wants to get in, they'll just have to wait. There's only room enough for two anyway. And even so, they have to be awfully good friends."

"We're nearly the last ones still up, anyway," Helen said.

"Here, have some." Patrice was bringing up a fleecy fistful of facial tissues from the case; she divided them with her friend.

"I missed these an awful lot on the Other Side. Couldn't get them for love nor money. I used to ask and ask, and they didn't know what I meant—"

She stopped and eyed her companion. "Oh, you have nothing to rub off, have you? Well, here, rub some of this on; then you'll have that to rub off."

Helen laughed. "You make me feel so giddy," she said with a wistful sort of admiration.

Patrice hunched her shoulders and grimaced impishly. "It's my last fling, sort of. From tomorrow night on I may have to be on my best behavior. Sober and sedate." She made a long face, and steepled her hands against her stomach, in mimicry of a bluenosed clergyman.

"Oh, on account of meeting your in-laws," Helen remembered.

"Hugh says they're not like that at all; I have absolutely nothing to worry about. But of course he just may be slightly prejudiced in their favor. I wouldn't think much of him if he wasn't."

She was scouring a mystic white circle on each cheek and then spreading them around, mouth open the whole while, though it played no part in the rite itself.

"Go ahead, help yourself," she invited. "Stick your finger in and dig out a gob. I'm not sure what it does for you, but it smells nice, so there's nothing to lose."

"Is that really true, what you told me?" Helen said, following suit. "That they've never even seen you until now? I can't believe it."

"Cross my heart and hope to die, they've never laid eyes on me in their lives. I met Hugh on the Other Side, like I told you this afternoon, and we were married over there, and we went on living over there until just now. My folks were dead, and I was on a scholarship, studying music, and he had a job with one of these government agencies; you know, one of these initialed outfits. They don't even know what I *look* like!"

"Didn't you even send them a picture of yourself? Not even after you were married?"

"We never even had a wedding picture taken; you know how us kids are nowadays. Biff, bing, bang! and we're married. I started to send them one of myself several times, but I was never quite satisfied with the ones I had. Self-conscious, you know; I wanted to make *such* a good first impression. One time Hugh even arranged a sitting for me at a photographer, and when I saw the proofs, I said, 'Over my dead body you'll send these!' Those French photographers! I knew I was going to meet them eventually, and snapshots are so—so— Anyway the ones *I* take. So finally I said to him, 'I've waited this long, I'm not going to send any to them at all now. I'll save it up for a surprise, let them see me in the flesh instead, when they finally do. That way, they won't build up any false hopes and then be disappointed.' I used to censor all his letters too, wouldn't let him describe me. You can imagine how he would have done it. *Mona Lisa, Venus on the Half Shell.* I'd say, 'No you don't!' when I'd catch him at it, and scratch it out. We'd have more tussles that way, chase each other around the room, trying to get the letter back or trying to get it away from me."

She became serious for a moment. Or at least, approached as closely to it as she seemed capable of.

"Y'know, now I wish I hadn't done that, sort of. Played hide-and-seek with them like this, I mean. Now I *have* got cold feet. Do you think they'll really like me? Suppose they don't? Suppose they have me built up in their expectations as someone entirely different, and—"

Like the little boy in the radio skit who prattles about a self-invented bugaboo until he ends up by frightening himself with it.

"How on earth do you make the water stay in this thing?" she interrupted herself. She pounded lightly on the plunger set into the washbasin. "Every time I get it to fill, it runs right out again."

"Twist it a little, and then push down on it, I think."

Patrice stripped off her wedding band before plunging her hands in. "Hold this for me. I want to wash my hands. I have a horror of losing it. It slipped down a drain on the Other Side, once, and they had to take out a whole section of pipe before they could get it out for me."

"It's beautiful," Helen said wistfully.

"Isn't it, though?" Patrice agreed. "See? It has our names, together, around it on the inside. Isn't that a cute idea? Keep it on your finger for me a minute. That's the safest."

"Isn't it supposed to be bad luck to do that? I mean, for you to take it off, and for me to put it on?"

Patrice tossed her head vaingloriously. "I *couldn't* have bad luck," she proclaimed. It was almost a challenge.

"And I," thought Helen somberly, "couldn't have good."

She watched it curiously as it slowly descended the length of her finger, easily, without forcing. There was a curiously familiar feeling to it, as of something that should have been there long ago, that belonged there and had been strangely lacking until now.

"So this is what it feels like," she said to herself poignantly.

The train pounded on, its headlong roar deadened, in here where they were, to a muted jittering.

Patrice stepped back, her toilette at last completed. "Well, this is my last night," she sighed. "By this time tomorrow night we'll already be there, the worst'll be over." She clasped her own arms, in a sort of half shiver of fright. "I hope they like what they're getting." She nervously stole a sidelong look at herself in the glass, primped at her hair.

"You'll be all right, Patrice," Helen reassured her quietly. "Nobody could help but like you."

Patrice crossed her fingers and held them up to show her. "Hugh says they're very well-off," she rambled on. "That makes it all the worse sometimes." She tittered in recollection. "I guess they must be. I know they even had to send us the money for the trip home. We were always on a shoestring, the whole time we were over there. We had an awful lot of fun, though. I think that's the only time you have fun, when you're on a shoestring, don't you?"

"Sometimes—you don't," remembered Helen, but she didn't answer.

"Anyway," her confidante babbled on, "as soon as they found out I was expecting, that did it! They wouldn't hear of my having my baby over there. I didn't much want to myself, as a matter of fact, and Hugh didn't want me to either. They should be born in the good old U.S.A., don't you think so? That's the least you can do for them."

"Sometimes that's *all* you can do for them," Helen thought wryly. "That—and seventeen cents."

She had finished now in turn.

Patrice urged, "Let's stay in here long enough to have a puff, now that we're here. We don't seem to be keeping anybody else out. And if we try to talk out there, they might shush us down; they're all trying to sleep." The little lighter-flame winked in coppery reflection against the mirrors and glistening chrome on all sides of them. She gave a sigh of heartfelt satisfaction. "I love these before-retiring talks with another girl. It's been ages since I last had one. Back in school, I guess. Hugh says I'm a woman's woman at heart." She stopped short and thought about it with a quizzical quirk of her head. "Is that good or bad? I must ask him."

Helen couldn't repress a smile. "Good, I guess. I wouldn't want to be a man's woman."

"I wouldn't either!" Patrice hastily concurred. "It always makes me think of someone who uses foul language and spits out of the corner of her mouth."

They both chuckled for a moment in unison. But Patrice's butterfly mind had already fluttered on to the next topic, as she dropped ash into the waste receptacle. "Wonder if I'll be able to smoke openly, once I'm home." She shrugged. "Oh well, there's always the back of the barn."

And then suddenly she had reverted to their mutual condition again.

"Are you frightened? About *it*, you know?"

Helen made the admission with her eyes.

"I am too." She took a reflective puff. "I think everyone is, a little, don't you? Men don't think we are. All I have to do is look at Hugh"—she deepened the dimple pits humorously—"and I can see he's frightened enough for the two of us, so then I don't let on that I'm frightened too. And *I* reassure *him*."

Helen wondered what it was like to have someone to talk to about it.

"Are *they* pleased about it?"

"Oh sure. They're tickled silly. First grandchild, you know. They didn't even ask us if we *wanted* to come back. 'You're coming back,' and that was that."

She pointed the remnant of her cigarette down toward one of the taps, quenched it with a sharp little jet of water.

"Ready? Shall we go back to our seats now?"

They were both doing little things. All life is that, the continuous doing of little things, all life long. And then suddenly a big thing strikes into their midst—and where are the little things, what became of them, what were they?

Her hand was to the door, reversing the little hand latch that Patrice had locked before, when they first came in. Patrice was somewhere behind her, replacing something in the uplidded dressing kit, about to close it and bring it with her. She could see her vaguely in the chromium sheeting lining the wall before her. Little things. Little things that life is made up of. Little things that stop—

Her senses played a trick on her. There was no time for them to synchronize with the thing that happened. They played her false. She had a fleeting impression, at first, of having done something wrong to the door, dislodged it in its entirety. Simply by touching that little hand latch. It was as though she were bringing the whole door slab down inward on herself. As though it were falling bodily out of its frame, hinges and all. And yet it never did, it never detached itself, it never came apart from the entire wall section it was imbedded in. So the second fleeting impression, equally false and equally a matter of seconds only, was that the entire wall of the compartment, door and all, was toppling, threatening to come down on her. And yet that never did either. Instead, the whole alcove seemed to upend, shift on a crazy axis, so that what had been the wall before her until now, had shifted to become the ceiling over her; so that what had been the floor she was standing on until now, had shifted to become the wall upright before her. The door was gone hopelessly out of reach, was a sealed trap overhead, impossible to attain.

The lights went. All light was gone, and yet so vividly explosive were the sensory images whirling through her mind that they glowed on of their own incandescence in the dark; it took her a comparatively long time to realize she was steeped in pitch-blackness, could no longer see physically. Only in afterglow of imaginative terror.

There was a nauseating sensation, as if the tracks, instead of being rigid steel rods, had softened into rippling ribbons, with the train still trying to follow their buckling curvature. The car seemed to go up and down, like a scenic railway performing foreshortened dips and rises that followed one another quicker and quicker and quicker. There was a distant rending, grinding, coming nearer, swelling as it came. It reminded her of a coffee mill they had had at home, when she was a little girl. But that one didn't draw you into its maw, crunching everything in sight, as this one was doing.

"Hugh!" the disembodied floor itself seemed to scream out behind her. Just once.

Then after that the floor fell silent.

There were minor impressions. Of seams opening, and of heavy metal partitions being bent together over her head, until the opening that held her was no longer foursquare, but tent-shaped. The darkness blanched momentarily in sudden ghostly pallor that was hot and puckery to breathe. Escaping steam. Then it thinned out again, and the darkness came back full-pitch. A little orange light flickered up somewhere, far off. Then that ebbed and dimmed again, and was gone too.

There wasn't any sound now, there wasn't any motion. Everything was still, and dreamy, and forgotten. What was this? Sleep? Death? She didn't think so. But it wasn't life either. She remembered life; life had been only a few minutes ago. Life had had lots of light in it, and people, and motion, and sound.

This must be something else. Some transitional stage, some other condition she hadn't been told about until now. Neither life, nor death, but something in between.

Whatever it was, it held pain in it; it was *all* pain, only pain. Pain that started small, and grew, and grew, and grew. She tried to move, and couldn't. A slim rounded thing, cold and sweating, down by her feet, was holding her down. It lay across her straight, like a water pipe sprung out of joint.

Pain that grew and grew. If she could have screamed, it might have eased it. But she couldn't seem to.

She put her hand to her mouth. On her third finger she encountered a little metal circlet, a ring that had been drawn over it. She bit on it. That helped, that eased it a little. The more the pain grew, the harder she bit.

She heard herself moan a little, and she shut her eyes. The pain went away. But it took everything else with it; thought, knowledge, awareness.

She opened her eyes again, reluctantly. Minutes? Hours? She didn't know. She only wanted to sleep, to sleep some more. Thought, knowledge, awareness, came back. But the pain didn't come back; that seemed to be gone for good. Instead, there was just this lassitude. She heard herself whimpering softly, like a small kitten. Or was it she?

She only wanted to sleep, to sleep some more. And they were making so much noise they wouldn't let her. Clanging, and pounding on sheets of loose tin, and prying things away. She rolled her head aside a little, in protest.

An attenuated shaft of light peered through, from somewhere up over her head. It was like a long thin finger, a spoke, prodding for her, pointing at her, trying to find her in the dark.

It didn't actually hit her, but it kept probing for her in all the wrong places, all around her.

She only wanted to sleep. She mewed a little in protest—or was it she?—and there was a sudden frightened flurry of activity, the pounding became faster, the prying became more hectic.

Then all of it stopped at once, there was a complete cessation, and a man's voice sounded directly over her, strangely hollow and blurred as when you talk through a tube.

"Steady. We're coming to you. Just a minute longer, honey. Can you hold out? Are you hurt? Are you bad? Are you alone under there?"

"No," she said feebly. "I've—I've just had a baby down here."

RECOVERY was like a progressive equalization of badly unbalanced solstices. At first, time was all nights, unbroken polar nights, with tiny fractional days lasting a minute or two at a time. Nights were sleep, and days were wakefulness. Then little by little the days expanded and the nights contracted. Presently, instead of many little days during the space of each twenty-four hours, there was just one long one in the middle of it each time, the way there should be. Soon this had even begun to overlap at one end, to continue beyond the setting of the sun and impinge into the first hour or two of evening. Now, instead of many little fragmentary days in the space of one night, there were many little fragmentary nights in the space of one day. Dozes or naps. The solstices had reversed themselves.

Recovery was on a second, concurrent plane as well. Dimension entered into it as well as duration. The physical size of her surroundings expanded along with the extension of her days. First there was just a small area around her that entered into awareness each time; the pillows behind her head, the upper third of the bed, a dim face just offside to her, bending down toward her, going away, coming back again. And over and above everything else, a small form allowed to nestle in her arms for a few moments at a time. Something that was alive and warm and hers. She came more alive then than at any other time. It was food and drink and sunlight; it was her lifeline back to life. The rest remained unfocused, lost in misty gray distances stretching out and around her.

But this core of visibility, this too expanded. Presently it had reached the foot of the bed. Then it had jumped over that, to the wide moat of the room beyond, its bottom hidden from sight. Then it had reached the walls of the room, on all three sides, and could go no further for the present; they stopped it. But that wasn't a limitation of inadequate awareness anymore; that was a limitation of physical equipment. Even well eyes were not made to go through walls.

It was a pleasant room. An infinitely pleasant room. This could not have been a haphazard effect achieved at random. It was too immediate, too all-pervading; every chord it struck was the right one: whether of color, proportion, acoustics, bodily tranquillity and well-being, and, above all, of personal security and sanctuary, of belonging somewhere at last, of having found a haven, a harbor, of being let be. The height of scientific skill and knowledge, therefore, must have entered into it, to achieve that cumulative effect that her mind could only label pleasant.

The overall effect was a warm, glowing ivory shade, not a chill, clinical white. There was a window over to her right, with a

Venetian blind. And when this was furled, the sun came through in a solid slab-like shaft, like a chunk of copper-gold ore. And when it was unfurled, the dismembered beams blurred and formed a hazy mist flecked with copper-gold motes that clung to the whole window like a halo. And still at other times they brought the slats sharply together and formed a cool blue dusk in the room, and even that was grateful, made you close your eyes without effort and take a nap.

There were always flowers standing there, too, over to her right, near the head of the bed. Never the same color twice. They must have been changed each day. They repeated themselves, but never in immediate succession. Yellow, and then the next day pink, and then the next day violet and white, and then the next day back to yellow again. She got so she looked for them. It made her want to open her eyes and see what color they would be this time. Maybe that was why they were there. The Face would bring them over and hold them closer for her to see, and then put them back again.

The first words she spoke each day were: "Let me see my little boy." But the second, or not far behind, were always: "Let me see my flowers."

And after a while there was fruit. Not right at first, but a little later on when she first began to enjoy appetite again. That was in a different place, not quite so close, over by the window. In a basket, with a big-eared satin bow standing up straight above its handle. Never the same fruit twice, that is to say, never the same arrangement or ratio of the various species, and never any slightest mark of spoilage, so she knew it must be new fruit each day. The satin bow was never the same twice, either, so presumably the basket was a different one too. A new basketful of fresh fruit each day.

And if it could never mean quite as much to her as the flowers, that is because flowers are flowers and fruit is fruit. It was still good to look at in its way. Blue grapes and green, and purple ones, with the sunlight shining through them and giving them a cathedral-window luster; Bartlett pears, with a rosy flush that almost belonged to apples on their yellow cheeks; plushy yellow peaches; pert little tangerines; apples that were almost purple in their apoplectic full-bloodedness.

Every day, nestled in cool, crisp, dark-green tissue.

She hadn't known that hospitals were so attentive. She hadn't known they provided such things for their patients; even patients who only had seventeen cents in their purses—or would have, had they had purses—when they were admitted.

She thought about the past sometimes, remembered it, reviewed it, the little there was of it. But it brought shadows into the room, dimmed its bright corners; it thinned even the thick girder-like shafts of sunlight coming through the window; it made her want the covers closer up around her shoulders, so she learned to avoid thinking of it, summoning it up.

She thought:

I was on a train. I was closeted in the washroom with another girl. She could remember the metallic sheen of the fixtures and the mirrors. She could see the other girl's face; three dimples in triangular arrangement, one on each cheek, one at the chin. She could even feel the shaking and vibration, the slight unsteadiness of footing, again, if she tried hard enough. But it made her slightly nauseated to do so, because she knew what was coming next, in a very few seconds. She knew now, but she hadn't known then. She usually snapped off the sensory image, as if it were a light switch, in a hurry at this point, to forestall what was surely coming next.

She remembered New York. She remembered the door that wouldn't open. She remembered the strip of one-way tickets falling out of an envelope. That was when the shadows really formed around, good and heavy. That was when the temperature of the room really went down. When she went back behind the train trip, to remember New York, on the other side of it.

She quickly shut her eyes and turned her head aside on the pillow, and shut the past out.

The present was kinder by far. And you could have it so easy, any given moment of the day. You could have it without trying at all. Stay in the present, let the present do. The present was safe. Don't stray out of it—not in either direction, forward or backward. Because there was only darkness, way out there all around it, and you didn't know what you'd find. Sit tight; lie tight, right where you were.

She opened her eyes and warmed to it again. The sunlight coming in, thick and warm and strong enough to carry the weight of a toboggan from the windowsill to the floor. The technicolored burst of flowers, the beribboned basket of fruit. The soothing quiet all around. They'd bring the little form in pretty soon, and let it nestle against her, and she'd know that happiness that was something new, that made you want to circle your arms and never let go.

Let the present do. Let the present last. Don't ask, don't seek, don't question, don't quarrel with it. Hang on to it for all you were worth.

IT WAS really the flowers that were her undoing, that brought the present to an end.

She wanted one of them one day. Wanted to separate one from the rest, and hold it in her hand, and smell its sweetness directly under her nose; it wasn't enough any longer just to enjoy them visually, to look at them in the abstract, in group formation.

They'd been moved nearer by this time. And she herself could move now more freely. She'd been lying quietly on her side admiring them for some time when the impulse formed.

There was a small one, dangling low, arching over in her direction, and she thought she'd get that. She turned more fully, so that she was completely sideward, and reached out toward it.

Her hand closed on its stalk, and it quivered delicately with the pressure. She knew she wouldn't have been able to break the stalk off short just with one hand alone, and she didn't want to do that anyway; didn't want to damage the flower, just borrow it for a while. So she started to withdraw the stalk vertically from the receptacle, and as it paid off and seemed never to come to an end, this swept her hand high upward and at last back over her own head.

It struck the bed-back, that part that was so close to her that she could never have seen it without making a complete head-turn, and something up there jiggled and quivered a little, as if threatening to detach itself and come down.

She made the complete head-turn, and even withdrew out from it a little, into a half-sitting position, something she had never attempted before, to bring it into focus.

It was a featherweight metal frame, a rectangle, clasped to the top bar of the bed, loose on its other three sides. Within was held a smooth mat of paper, with fine neat writing on it that blurred until it had stopped the slight swaying that her impact had set in motion.

It had been inches from her head, just over her head, all this time, but she'd never seen it until now.

Her chart.

She peered at it intently.

Suddenly the present and all its safety exploded into fragments, and the flower fell from her extended hand onto the floor.

There were three lines at the top, in neat symmetry. The first part of each was printed and left incomplete; the rest was finished out in typescript.

It said at the top, "Section—"
And then it said, "Maternity."
It said below that, "Room—"
And then it said, "25."
It said at the bottom, "Patient's Name—"
And then it said, "Hazzard, Patrice (Mrs.)."

THE nurse opened the door, and her face changed. The smile
died off on it. You could detect the change in her face from all the
way over there, even before she'd come any closer to the bed.

She came over and took her patient's temperature. Then she
straightened the chart.

Neither of them said anything.

There was fear in the room. There was shadow in the room.
The present was no longer in the room. The future had taken its
place. Bringing fear, bringing shadow, bringing strangeness; worse
than even the past could have brought.

The nurse held the thermometer toward the light and scanned
it. Then her brows deepened. She put the thermometer down.

She asked the question carefully, as though she had gauged its tone and its tempo before allowing herself to ask it. She said, "What happened? Has something upset you? You're running a slight temperature."

The girl in the bed answered with a question of her own. Frightenedly, tautly. "What's that doing on my bed? Why is it there?"

"Everyone who's ill has to have one," the nurse answered soothingly. "It's nothing, just a—"

"But look—the name. It says—"

"Does the sight of your own name frighten you? You mustn't look at it. You're really not supposed to see it there. Sh, don't talk now anymore."

"But there's something I— But you have to tell me, I don't understand—"

The nurse took her pulse.

And as she did so, the patient was suddenly looking at her own hand, in frozen, arrested horror. At the little circlet with diamonds, enfolding the third finger. At the wedding band. As though she'd never seen it before, as though she wondered what it was doing there.

The nurse saw her trying to take it off, with flurried little tugs. It wouldn't move easily.

The nurse's face changed. "Just a moment, I'll be right back," she said uneasily.

She brought the doctor in with her. Her whispering stopped as they crossed the threshold.

He came over to the bed, put his hand to her forehead.

He nodded to the nurse and said, "Slight."

He said, "Drink this."

It tasted salty.

They put the hand under the covers, out of sight. The hand with the ring on it.

They took the glass from her lips. She didn't want to ask any questions anymore. She did, but some other time, not right now. There was something they had to be told. She'd had it a minute ago, but now it had escaped her again.

She sighed. Some other time, but not right now. She didn't want to do anything right now but sleep.

She turned her face toward the pillow and slept.

IT CAME right back again. The first thing. With the first glimpse of the flowers, the first glimpse of the fruit, right as her eyelids first went up and the room came into being. It came right back again.

Something said to her: Tread softly, speak slow. Take care, take care. She didn't know what or why, but she knew it must be heeded.

The nurse said to her, "Drink your orange juice."

The nurse said to her, "You can have a little coffee in your milk, starting from today on. Each day a little more. Won't that be a pleasant change?"

Tread softly, speak with care.

She said, "What happened to—"

She took another sip of beige-colored milk. Tread warily, speak slow.

"To whom?" The nurse finally completed it for her.

Oh, careful now, careful. "There was another girl in the train washroom with me. Is she all right?" She took another sip of milk for punctuation. Hold the glass steady, now; that's right. Don't let it shake. Down to the tray again, even and slow; that's it.

The nurse shook her head reticently. She said, "No."

"She's dead?"

The nurse wouldn't answer. She too was treading softly. She too felt her way. She too wouldn't rush in. She said, "Did you know her very well?"

"No."

"You'd only met her on the train?"

"Only on the train."

The nurse had paved her own way now. It was safe to proceed. The nurse nodded. She was answering the question two sentences before, by delayed action. "She's gone," she said quietly.

The nurse watched her face expectantly. The pavement held; there was no cave-in.

The nurse ventured a step farther.

"Isn't there anyone else you want to ask about?"

"What happened to—?"

The nurse took the tray away, as if stripping the scene for a crisis.

"To *him?*"

Those were the words. She adopted them. "What happened to him?"

The nurse said, "Just a moment." She went to the door, opened it, and motioned to someone unseen.

The doctor came in, and a second nurse. They stood waiting, as if prepared to meet an emergency.

The first nurse said, "Temperature normal." She said, "Pulse normal."

The second nurse was mixing something in a glass.

The first nurse, her own, stood close to the bed. She took her by the hand and held it tightly. Just held it like that, tight and unyielding.

The doctor nodded.

The first nurse moistened her lips. She said, "Your husband wasn't saved either, Mrs. Hazzard."

She could feel her face pale with shock. The skin pulled as though it were a size too small.

She said, "No, there's something wrong. No, you're making a mistake—"

The doctor motioned unobtrusively. He and the second nurse closed in on her swiftly.

Somebody put a cool hand on her forehead, held her pressed downward, kindly but firmly; she couldn't tell whose it was.

She said, "No, please let me tell you!"

The second nurse was holding something to her lips. The first one was holding her hand, tight and warm, as if to say, "I am here. Don't be frightened, I am here." The hand on her forehead was cool but competent. It was heavy, but not too heavy; just persuasive enough to make her head lie still.

"Please—" she said listlessly.

She didn't say anything more after that. They didn't either.

Finally she overheard the doctor murmur, as if in punctuation, "She stood that very well."

IT CAME back again. How could it fail to now? You cannot sleep at all times, only at small times. And with it came: Tread softly, speak with care.

The nurse's name was Miss Allmeyer, the one she knew best.

"Miss Allmeyer, does the hospital give everyone those flowers every day?"

"We'd like to, but we couldn't afford it. Those flowers cost five dollars each time you see them. They're just for you."

"Is it the hospital that supplies that fruit every day?"

The nurse smiled gently. "We'd like to do that too. We only wish we could. That fruit cost ten dollars a basket each time you see it. It's a standing order, just for you."

"Well, who—" Speak softly.

The nurse smiled winningly. "Can't you guess, honey? That shouldn't be very hard."

"There's something I want to tell you. Something you must let me tell you." She turned her head restlessly on the pillows, first to one side, then the other, then back to the first.

"Now, honey, are we going to have a bad day? I thought we were going to have such a good day."

"Could you find out something for me?"

"I'll try."

"The handbag, the handbag that was in the train washroom with me. How much was in it?"

"*Your* handbag?"

"The handbag. The one that was there when I was in there."

The nurse came back later and said, "It's safe; it's being held for you. About fifty dollars or so."

That wasn't hers; that was the other one.

"There were two."

"There is another," the nurse admitted. "It doesn't belong to anyone now." She looked down commiseratingly. "There was just seventeen cents in it," she breathed almost inaudibly.

She didn't have to be told that. She knew by heart. She remembered from before boarding the train. She remembered from the train itself. Seventeen cents. Two pennies, a nickel, a dime.

"Could you bring the seventeen cents here? Could I have it just to look at it? Could I have it here next to the bed?"

The nurse said, "I'm not sure it's good for you, to brood like that. I'll see what they say."

She brought it, though, inside a small envelope.

She was alone with it. She dumped the four little coins from the envelope into the palm of her hand. She closed her hand upon them tightly, held them gripped like that, fiercely, in a knot of dilemma.

Fifty dollars, symbolically. Symbol of an untold amount more.

Seventeen cents, literally. Symbol of nothing, for there wasn't any more. Seventeen cents and nothing else.

The nurse came back again and smiled at her. "Now, what was it you said you wanted to tell me?"

She returned the smile wanly. "It can keep for a while longer. I'll tell you some other time. Tomorrow, maybe, or the next day. Not—not right today."

THERE was a letter on the breakfast tray.

The nurse said, "See? Now you're beginning to get mail, just like the well people do."

It was slanted toward her, leaning against the milk glass. On the envelope it said:

Mrs. Patrice Hazzard

She was frightened of it. She couldn't take her eyes off it. The glass of orange juice shook in her hand. The writing on it seemed to get bigger, and bigger, and bigger, as it stood there.

MRS. PATRICE HAZZARD

"Open it," the nurse encouraged her. "Don't just look at it like that. It won't bite you."

She tried to twice, and twice it fell. The third time she managed to rip one seam along its entire length.

> Patrice, dear:
>
> Though we've never seen you, you're our daughter now, dear. You're Hugh's legacy to us. You're all we have now, you and the little fellow. I can't come to you, where you are; doctor's orders. The shock was too much for me, and he forbids my making the trip. You'll have to come to us, instead. Come soon, dear. Come home to us, in our loneliness and loss. It will make it that much easier to bear. It won't be long now, dear. We've been in constant touch with Dr. Brett, and he sends very encouraging reports of your progress—

The rest didn't matter so much; she let it fade from her attention.

It was like train wheels going through her head.

Though we've never seen you.

Though we've never seen you.

Though we've never seen you.

The nurse eased it from her forgetful fingers after a while and put it back in its envelope. She watched the nurse fearfully as she moved about the room.

"If I weren't Mrs. Hazzard, would I be allowed to stay in this room?"

The nurse laughed cheerfully. "We'd put you out, we'd throw you right outside into one of the wards," she said, bending close toward her in mock threat.

The nurse said, "Here, take your young son."

She held him tightly, in fierce, almost convulsive protectiveness.

Seventeen cents. Seventeen cents lasts such a short time, goes such a short way.

The nurse felt in good humor. She tried to prolong their little joke of a moment ago. "Why? Are you trying to tell me you're not Mrs. Hazzard?" she asked banteringly.

She held him fiercely, protectively close.

Seventeen cents, seventeen cents.

"No," she said in a smothered voice, burying her face against him, "I'm not trying to tell you that. I'm not trying."

.

12

SHE was in a dressing robe, sitting by the window in the sun. It was quilted blue silk. She wore it every day when she got up out of bed. On the breast pocket it had a monogram embroidered in white silk—the letters "PH" intertwined. There were slippers to match.

She was reading a book. On the flyleaf, though she was long past it, it was inscribed "To Patrice, with love from Mother H." There was a row of other books on the stand beside the bed. Ten or twelve of them; books with vivacious jackets, turquoise, magenta, vermilion, cobalt, and with vivacious, lighthearted contents to match. Not a shadow between their covers.

There was a scattering of orange peel, and two or three seeds, in a dish on a low stand beside her easy chair. There was a cigarette burning in another, smaller dish beside that one. It was custom-made, it had a straw tip, and the initials "PH" on it had not yet been consumed.

The sunlight, falling from behind and over her, made her hair seem hazily translucent, made it almost seem like golden foam about her head. It skipped the front of her, from there on down, due to the turn of the chair-back, and struck again in a little golden pool across one outthrust bare instep, lying on it like a warm, luminous kiss.

There was a light tap at the door, and the doctor came in.

He drew out a chair and sat down facing her, leaving its straight back in front of him as an added note of genial informality.

"I hear you're leaving us soon."

The book fell, and he had to pick it up for her. He offered it back to her, but when she seemed incapable of taking it, he put it aside on the stand.

"Don't look so frightened. Everything's arranged—"

She had a little difficulty with her breathing. "Where—? Where to?"

"Why, home, of course."

She put her hand to her hair and flattened it a little, but then it sprang up again, gaseous as before, in the sun.

"Here are your tickets." He took an envelope out of his pocket, tried to offer it to her. Her hands withdrew a little, each one around a side of the chair toward the back. He put the envelope between the pages of the discarded book finally, leaving it outthrust like a place mark.

Her eyes were very large. Larger than they had seemed before he came into the room. "When?" she said with scarcely any breath at all.

"Wednesday, the early afternoon train."

Suddenly panic was licking all over her, like a shriveling, congealing, frigid flame.

"No, I can't! No! Doctor, you've got to listen—!" She tried to grab his hand with both of hers and hold on to it.

He spoke to her playfully, as if she were a child. "Now, now, here. What's all this? What *is* all this?"

"No, Doctor, no!" She shook her head insistently.

He sandwiched her hand between both of his and held it that way, consolingly. "I understand," he said soothingly. "We're a little shaky yet. We've just finished getting used to things as they are. We're a little timid about giving up familiar surroundings for those that are strange to us. We all have it; it's a typical nervous reaction. Why, you'll be over it in no time."

"But I can't *do* it, Doctor," she whispered passionately. "I can't *do* it."

He chucked her under the chin, to instill courage in her. "We'll put you on the train, and all you have to do is ride. Your family will be waiting to take you off at the other end."

"My family."

"Don't make such a face about it," he coaxed whimsically.

He glanced around at the crib.

"What about the young man here?"

He went over to it and lifted the child out, brought him to her, and put him in her arms.

"You want to take him home, don't you? You don't want him to grow up in a hospital?" He laughed at her teasingly. "You want him to *have* a home, don't you?"

She held him to her, lowered her head to him.

"Yes," she said at last, submissively. "Yes, I want him to have a home."

13

A TRAIN again. But how different it was now. No crowded aisles, no jostling figures, no flux of patient, swaying humanity. A compartment, a roomette all to herself. A little table on braces that could go up, that could go down. A closet with a full-length mirrored door, just as in any ground-fast little dwelling. On the rack the neat luggage in recessive tiers, brand-new, in use now for the first time, glossy patent finish, hardware glistening, "PH" trimly stenciled in vermilion on the rounded corners. A little shaded lamp to read by when the countryside grew dark. Flowers in a holder, going-away flowers—no, coming-homeward flowers—presented by proxy at the point of departure; glazed fruit candies in a box; a magazine or two.

And outside the two wide windows that formed almost a single panel from wall to wall, trees sailing peacefully by, off a way in a single line, dappled with sunshine—dark green on one side, light apple green on the other. Clouds sailing peacefully by, only a little more slowly than the trees, as if the two things worked on separate, yet almost synchronized, belts of continuous motion. Meadows and fields, and the little ripples that hillocks made off in the distance every once in a while. Going up a little, coming down again. The wavy line of the future.

And on the seat opposite her own, and more important by far than all this, snug in a little blue blanket, small face still, small eyes closed—something to cherish, something to love. All there was in the world to love. All there was to go on for, along that wavy line outside.

Yes, how different it was now. And—how infinitely preferable the first time had been to this one. Fear rode with her now.

There hadn't been fear then. There hadn't been a seat, there hadn't been a bite to eat, there had only been seventeen cents. And just ahead, unguessed, rushing ever nearer with the miles, there had been calamity, horror, the beating of the wings of death.

But there hadn't been fear. There hadn't been this gnawing inside. There hadn't been this strain and counterstrain, this pulling one way and pulling the other. There had been the calm, the certainty, of going along the right way, the only way there was to go.

The wheels chattered, as they always chatter, on every train that has ever run. But saying now, to her ear alone:

> "You'd better go back, you'd better go back,
> Clicketty-clack, clicketty-clack,
> Stop while you can, you still can go back."

A very small part of her moved, the least part of her moved. Her thumb unbracketed, and her four fingers opened slowly, and the tight white knot they'd made for hours past dissolved. There in its center, exposed now—

An Indian-head penny.

A Lincoln-head penny.

A buffalo nickel.

A Liberty-head dime.

Seventeen cents. She even knew the dates on them by heart by now.

> "Clicketty-clack,
> Stop and go back,
> You still have the time,
> Turn and go back."

Slowly the fingers folded up and over again; the thumb crossed over and locked them in place.

Then she took the whole fist and struck it distractedly against her forehead and held it there for a moment where it had struck.

She stood up suddenly, and tugged at one of the pieces of luggage, and swiveled it around, so that its outermost corner was now inward. The "PH" disappeared. Then she did it to the piece below. The second "PH" disappeared.

The fear wouldn't disappear. It wasn't just stenciled on a corner of her; it was all over her.

There was a light knock outside the door, and she started as violently as though it had been a resounding crash.

"Who's there?" she gasped.

A porter's voice answered, "Five mo' minutes fo' Caulfield."

She reared from the seat and ran to the door, flung it open. He was already going down the passage. "No, wait! It can't be—"

"It sho' enough is, though, ma'm."

"So quickly, though. I didn't think—"

He smiled back at her indulgently. "It always comes between Clarendon and Hastings. That's the right place fo' it. And we've had Clarendon already, and Hastings's comin' right after it. Ain't never change since I been on this railroad."

She closed the door, and swung around, and leaned her whole back against it, as if trying to keep out some catastrophic intrusion.

"Too late to go back,
Too late to go back—"

"I can still ride straight through. I can ride past without getting off," she thought. She ran to the windows and peered out ahead, at an acute angle, as if the oncoming sight of it in itself would resolve her difficulty in some way.

Nothing yet. It was coming on very gradually. A house, all by itself. Then another house, still all by itself. Then a third. They were beginning to come thicker now.

"Ride straight through. Don't get off at all. They can't make you. Nobody can. Do this one last thing. That's all there's time for now."

She ran back to the door and hurriedly turned the little finger latch under the knob, locking it on the inside.

The houses were coming in more profusion, but they were coming slower too. They didn't sail anymore; they dawdled. A school building drifted by; you could tell what it was even from afar. Spotless, modern, brand-new-looking, its concrete function-alism gleaming spic-and-span in the sun, copiously glassed. She could even make out small swings in motion, in the playground beside it. She glanced aside at the small blanketed bundle on the seat. That would be the kind of school she'd want—

She didn't speak, but her own voice was loud in her ears. "Help me, somebody; I don't know what to do!"

The wheels were dying, as though they'd run out of lubrication. Or like a phonograph record that runs down.

Cli-ck, cla-ck,
Cli-i-ck, cla-a-a-ck.

Each revolution seemed about to be the last.

Suddenly a long shed started up, just outside the windows, running along parallel to them, and then a white sign suspended from it started to go by, letter by letter in reverse.

D-L-E-I-

It got to the F, and it stuck. It wouldn't budge. She all but screamed. The train had stopped.

A knock sounded right behind her back, the vibration of it seeming to go through her chest.

"Caulfield, ma'm."

Then someone tried the knob.

"Help you with yo' things?"

Her clenched fist tightened around the seventeen cents, until the knuckles showed white and livid with the pressure.

She ran to the seat and picked up the blue blanket and what it held.

There were people out there, just on the other side of the window. Their heads were low, but she could see them, and they could see her. There was a woman looking right at her.

Their eyes met; their eyes locked, held fast. She couldn't turn her head away, she couldn't withdraw deeper into the compartment. It was as though those eyes riveted her where she stood.

The woman pointed to her. She called out in jubilation, for the benefit of someone else, unseen. "There she is! I've found her! Here, this car up here!"

She raised her hand, and she waved. She waved to the little somnolent, blinking head coifed in the blue blanket, looking solemnly out the window. Made her fingers flutter in that special wave you give to very small babies.

The look on her face couldn't have been described. It was as when life begins all over again, after an interruption, a hiatus. It was as when the sun peers through again at the end, at the end of a bleak wintry day.

The girl holding the baby put her head down close to his, almost as if averting it from the window. Or as if they were communing together, exchanging some confidence in secret, to the exclusion of everyone else.

She was.

"For you," she breathed. "For you. And God forgive me."

Then she carried him over to the door with her and turned the latch to let the harassed porter in.

SOMETIMES there is a dividing line running across life. Sharp, almost actual, like the black stroke of a paintbrush or the white gash of a chalk mark. Sometimes, but not often.

For her there was. It lay somewhere along those few yards of car passage, between the compartment window and the car steps, where for a moment or two she was out of sight of those standing waiting outside. One girl left the window. Another girl came down the steps. A world ended, and another world began.

She wasn't the girl who had been holding her baby by the compartment window just now.

Patrice Hazzard came down those car steps.

Frightened, tremulous, very white in the face, but Patrice Hazzard.

She was aware of things, but only indirectly; she only had eyes for those other eyes looking into hers from a distance of a few inches away. All else was background. Behind her back the train glided on. Bearing with it its hundreds of living passengers. And, all unknown, in an empty compartment, a ghost. Two ghosts, a large one and a very small one.

Forever homeless now, never to be retrieved.

The hazel eyes came in even closer to hers. They were kind; they smiled around the edges; they were gentle, tender. They hurt a little. *They were trustful.*

She was in her fifties, their owner. Her hair was softly graying, and only underneath had the process been delayed. She was as tall as Patrice and as slim, and she shouldn't have been, for it wasn't the slimness of fashionable effort or artifice, and something about her clothes revealed it to be recent, only the past few months.

But even these details about her were background, and the man of her own age standing just past her shoulder was background too. It was only her face that was immediate, and the eyes in her face, so close now. Saying so much without a sound.

She placed her hands lightly upon Patrice's cheeks, one on each, framing her face between them in a sort of accolade, a sacramental benison.

Then she kissed her on the lips, in silence, and there was a life-time in the kiss; the girl could sense it. The lifetime of a man. The many years it takes to raise a man, from childhood, through boyhood, into a grown son. There was bitter loss in the kiss, the loss of all that at a single blow. The end for a time of all hope, and weeks of cruel grief. But then too there was the reparation of loss, the finding of a daughter, the starting over with another, a smaller son. No, with the same son, the same blood, the same flesh. Only going back and starting again from the beginning, in sweeter, sadder sponsorship this time, forewarned by loss. And there was the burgeoning of hope anew.

There were all those things in it. They were spoken in it; they were felt in it. And they were meant to be felt in it; they had been put into it for that purpose.

This was not a kiss under a railroad-station shed; it was a sacrament of adoption.

Then she kissed the child. And smiled as you do at your own. And a little crystal drop that hadn't been there before was resting on its small pink cheek.

The man came forward and kissed her on the forehead. "I'm Father, Patrice."

He stooped, and straightened, and said, "I'll take your things over to the car." A little glad to escape from an emotional moment, as men are apt to be.

The woman hadn't said a word. In all the moments she'd been standing before her, not a word had passed her lips. She saw, perhaps, the pallor in her face; could read the shrinking, the uncertainty, in her eyes.

She put her arms about her and drew her to her now, in a warmer, more mundane, more everyday greeting than the one that had passed before. Drew the girl's head to rest upon her own shoulder for a moment. And as she did so, she spoke for the first time, low in her ear, to give her courage, to give her peace.

"You're home, Patrice. Welcome home, dear."

And in those few words, so simply said, so inalterably meant, Patrice Hazzard knew she had found at last all the goodness there is or ever can be in this world.

15

AND so this was what it was like to be home, to be in a home of your own, in a room of your own.

She had another dress on now, ready to go down to table. She sat there in a wing chair waiting, very straight, looking a little small against its outspread back. Her back was up against it very straight, her legs dropped down to the floor very straight and meticulously side by side. She had her hand out resting on the crib, the crib they'd bought for him and that she'd found already here waiting when she first entered the room. He was in it now. They'd even thought of that.

They'd left her alone; she would have had to be alone to savor it as fully as she was doing. Still drinking it in, hours after;

basking in it, inhaling the essence of it; there was no word for what it did to her. Hours after; and her head every now and then would still give that slow, comprehensive, marveling sweep around from side to side, taking in all four walls of it. And even up overhead, not forgetting the ceiling. A roof over your head. A roof to keep out rain and cold and loneliness— Not just the anonymous roof of a rented building, no; the roof of home. Guarding you, sheltering you, keeping you, watching over you.

And somewhere downstairs, dimly perceptible to her acutely attuned ears, the soothing bustle of an evening meal in preparation. Carried to her in faint snatches now and then at the opening of a door, stilled again at its closing. Footsteps busily crossing an uncarpeted strip of wooden floor, then coming back again. An occasional faint clash of crockery or china. Once even the voice of the colored housekeeper, for an instant of bugle-like clarity. "No, it ain't ready yet, Miz' Hazzard; need five mo' minutes."

And the laughingly protesting admonition that followed, miraculously audible as well: "Sh, Aunt Josie. We have a baby in the house now; he may be napping."

Someone was coming up the stairs now. They were coming up the stairs now to tell her. She shrank back a little in the chair. Now she was a little frightened, a little nervous again. Now there would be no quick escape from the moment's confrontation, as at the railroad station. Now came the real meeting, the real blending, the real taking into the fold. Now was the real test.

"Patrice dear, supper's ready whenever you are."

You take *supper* in the evening, when you're home, in your own home. When you go out in public or to someone else's home, you may take *dinner.* But in the evening, in your own home, it's *supper* you take, and never anything else. Her heart was as fiercely glad as though the trifling word were a talisman. She remembered when she was a little girl, those few brief years that had ended so quickly— The call to *supper*, only *supper*, never anything else.

She jumped from the chair and ran over and opened the door. "Shall I—shall I bring him down with me or leave him up here in the crib till I come back?" she asked, half eagerly, half uncertainly. "I fed him already at five, you know."

Mother Hazzard slanted her head coaxingly. "Ah, why don't you bring him down with you just tonight, anyway? It's the first night. Don't hurry, dear; take your time."

When she came out of the room holding him in her arms moments later, she stopped a moment, fingered the edge of the door lingeringly. Not where the knob was, but up and down the unbroken surface where there was no knob.

Watch over my room for me, she breathed unheard. I'm coming right back. Take care of it. Don't let anyone— Will you?

She would come down these same stairs many hundreds of times to come, she knew, as she started down them now. She would come down them fast. She would come down them slowly. She would come down them blithely, in gaiety. And perhaps she might come down them in fear, in trouble. But now, tonight, this was the very first time of all that she was coming down them.

She held him close to her and felt her way, for they were new to her; she hadn't got the measure of them, the feel of them yet, and she didn't want to miss her step.

They were standing about in the dining room waiting for her. Not rigidly, formally, like drill sergeants, but in unselfconscious ease, as if unaware of the small tribute of consideration they were giving her. Mother Hazzard was leaning forward, giving a last-minute touch to the table, shifting something a little. Father

Hazzard was looking up toward the lights through the spectacles with which he'd just been reading, and polishing them off before returning them to their case. And there was a third person in the room, somebody with his back half to her at the moment of entrance, surreptitiously pilfering a salted peanut from a dish on the buffet.

He turned forward again and threw it away when he heard her come in. He was young and tall and friendly-looking, and his hair was— A camera shutter clicked in her mind, and the film rolled on.

"There's the young man!" Mother Hazzard reveled. "There's the young man himself! Here, give him to me. You know who this is, of course." And then she added, as though it were wholly unnecessary even to qualify it by so much, "Bill."

But who—? she wondered. They hadn't said anything until now.

He came forward, and she didn't know what to do, he was so close to her own age. She half offered her hand, hoping that if it was too formal, the gesture would remain unnoticed.

He took it, but he didn't shake it. Instead, he pressed it between both of his, held it warmly buried like that for a moment or two.

"Welcome home, Patrice," he said quietly. And there was something about the straight, unwavering look in his eyes as he said it that made her think she'd never heard anything said so sincerely, so simply, so loyally, before.

And that was all. Mother Hazzard said, "You sit here, from now on."

Father Hazzard said unassumingly, "We're very happy, Patrice," and sat down at the head of the table.

Whoever Bill was, he sat down opposite her.

The colored housekeeper peeked through the door for a minute and beamed. "Now this look right! This what that table been needing. This just finish off that empty si—"

Then she quickly checked herself, clapping a catastrophic hand to her mouth, and whisked from sight again.

Mother Hazzard glanced down at her plate for a second, then immediately looked up again smiling, and the hurt was gone, had not been allowed to linger.

They didn't say anything memorable. You don't say anything memorable across the tables of home. Your heart speaks, and not your brain, to the other hearts around you. She forgot after a while to notice what she was saying, to weigh, to reckon it. That's what home is, what home should be. It flowed from her as easily as it did from them. She knew that was what they were trying to do for her. And they were succeeding. Strangeness was already gone with the soup, never to return. Nothing could ever bring it back again. Other things could come—she hoped they wouldn't. But never strangeness, the unease of unfamiliarity, again. They had succeeded.

"I hope you don't mind the white collar on that dress, Patrice. I purposely saw to it there was a touch of color on everything I picked out. I didn't want you to be too—"

"Oh, some of those things are so lovely. I really hadn't seen half of them myself until I unpacked just now."

"The only thing that I was afraid of was the sizes, but that nurse of yours sent me a complete—"

"She took a tape measure all over me one day, I remember that now, but she wouldn't tell me what it was for—"

"Which kind for you, Patrice? Light or dark?"

"It really doesn't—"

"No, tell him just this once, dear; then after that he won't have to ask you."

"Dark, then, I guess."

"You and me both."

He spoke a little less frequently than the remaining three of them. Just a touch of shyness, she sensed. Not that he was strained or tongue-tied or anything. Perhaps it was just his way; he had a quiet, unobtrusive way.

The thing was, who exactly was he? She couldn't ask outright now any longer. She'd omitted to at the first moment, and now it was twenty minutes too late for that. No last name had been given, so he must be—

I'll find out soon, she reassured herself. I'm bound to. She was no longer afraid.

Once, she found he'd just been looking at her when her eyes went to him, and she wondered what he'd been thinking while doing so. And yet not to have admitted that she knew, that she could tell by the lingering traces of his expression, would have been to lie to herself. He'd been thinking that her face was pleasant, that he liked it.

And then after a little while he said, "Dad, pass the bread over this way, will you?"

And then she knew who he was.

EPISCOPAL Church of St. Bartholomew, social kingpin among all
the churches of Caulfield, on a golden April Sunday morning.

She stood there by the font, child in her arms, immediate family and their close friends gathered beside her.

They had insisted upon this. She hadn't wanted it. Twice she
had postponed it, for two Sundays in succession now, after all
the arrangements had been made. First, by pleading a cold that
she did not really have. Secondly, by pleading a slight one that the
child actually did have. Today she hadn't been able to postpone it
any longer. They would have finally sensed the deliberation
underlying her excuses.

She kept her head down, hearing the ceremony rather than

seeing it. As though afraid to look on openly at it. As though afraid of being struck down momentarily at the feet of all of them for her blasphemy.

She had on a broad-brimmed hat of semi-transparent horsehair and that helped her, veiling her eyes and the upper part of her face when she cast it down like that.

Mournful memories, they probably thought. Grief-stricken.

Guilty, in reality. Scandalized. Not brazen enough to gaze at this mockery unabashed.

Arms reached out toward her, to take the child from her. The godmother's arms. She gave him over, trailing the long lace ceremonial gown that—she had almost said "his father"—that a stranger named Hugh Hazzard had worn before him, and that *his* father, Donald, had worn before *him.*

Her arms felt strangely empty after that. She wanted to cross them protectively over her breast, as though she were unclad. She forced herself not to with an effort. It was not her form that was unclad, it was her conscience. She dropped them quietly, clasped them before her, looked down.

"Hugh Donald Hazzard, I baptize thee—"

They had gone through the parody of consulting her preferences in this. To her it was a parody; not to them. She wanted him named after Hugh, of course? Yes, she had said demurely, after Hugh. Then how about the middle name? After her own father? Or perhaps two middle names, one for each grandfather? (She actually hadn't been able to recall her own father's name at the moment; it came back to her sometime after, not without difficulty. Mike: a scarcely remembered figure of a looming longshoreman, killed in a drunken brawl on the Embarcadero when she was ten.)

One middle name would do. After Hugh's father, she had said demurely.

She could feel her face burning now, knew it must be flushed with shame. They mustn't see that. She kept it steadily down.

"—in the name of the Father, and of the Son, and of the Holy Ghost. Amen."

The minister sprinkled water on the child's head. She could see a stray drop or two fall upon the floor, darken into coin dots. A dime, a nickel, two pennies. Seventeen cents.

The infant began to wail in protest, as numberless infants before it since time immemorial. The infant from a New York furnished rooming house who had become heir to the first, the wealthiest family in Caulfield, in all the county, maybe even in all that state.

"You have nothing to cry about," she thought morosely.

THERE was a cake for him, on his first birthday, with a single candle standing defiantly in the middle of it, its flame like a yellow butterfly hovering atop a fluted white column. They made great to-do and ceremony about the little immemorial rites that went with it. The first grandson. The first milestone.

"But if he can't make the wish," she demanded animatedly, "is it all right if I make it for him? Or doesn't that count?"

Aunt Josie, the cake's creator, instinctively deferred to in all such matters of lore, nodded pontifically from the kitchen doorway. "You make it for him, honey; he git it just the same," she promised.

Patrice dropped her eyes, and her face sobered for a moment.

Peace, all your life. Safety, such as this. Your own around you always, such as now. And for myself—from you, someday—forgiveness.

"You got it? Now blow."

"Him or me?"

"It count just like for him."

She leaned down, pressed her cheek close to his, and blew softly. The yellow butterfly fluttered agitatedly, shriveled into nothingness.

"Now cut," coached the self-imposed mistress of ceremonies.

She closed his chubby little hand around the knife handle, enfolded it with her own, and tenderly guided it. The mystic incision made, she touched her finger to the sugary icing, scraped off a tiny crumb, and then placed it to his lips.

A great crowing and cooing went up, as though they had all just been witnesses to a prodigy of precocity.

A lot of people had come in; they hadn't had so many people all in the house at one time since she'd first been there. And long after the small honor guest had been withdrawn from the scene and taken upstairs to bed, the festivities continued under their own momentum, even accelerated somewhat. In that way grownups have of appropriating a child's party, given the slightest encouragement.

She came down again, afterward, to the lighted, bustling rooms, and moved about among them, chatting, smiling, happier tonight than she ever remembered being before. A cup of punch in one hand, in the other a sandwich with one bite gone, that she never seemed to get around to taking a second bite out of. Every time she raised it toward her mouth somebody said something to her, or she said something to somebody. It didn't matter; it was more fun that way.

Bill brushed by her once, grinning. "How does it feel to be an *old* mother?"

"How does it feel to be an *old* uncle?" she rejoined pertly over her shoulder.

A year ago seemed a long time away; just a year ago tonight, with its horror and its darkness and its fright. That hadn't happened to her; it *couldn't* have. That had happened to a girl named— No, she didn't want to remember that name, she didn't even want to summon it back for a fleeting instant. It had nothing to do with her.

"Aunt Josie's sitting up there with him. No, he'll be all right; he's a very *good* baby about going to sleep."

"Coming from a detached observer."

"Well, I *am* detached at this minute, so I'm entitled to say so. He's all the way upstairs, and I'm down here."

She was in the brightly lighted living room of her home, here, with her friends, her family's friends, all gathered about her, laughing and chatting. A year ago was more than a long time away. It had never happened. No, it had never happened. Not to her, anyway.

A great many of the introductions were blurred. There were so many firsts, on an occasion like this. She looked about, dutifully recapitulating the key people, as befitted her role of assistant hostess. Edna Harding and Marilyn Bryant, they were those two girls sitting one on each side of Bill, and vying with one another for his attention. She suppressed a mischievous grin. Look at him, sober-faced as a totem pole. Why, it was enough to turn his head—if he hadn't happened to have a head that was unturnable by girls, as far as she'd been able to observe. Guy Ennis was that dark-haired young man over there getting someone a punch cup;

he was easy to memorize because he'd come in alone. Some old friend of Bill's, evidently. Funny that the honeybees didn't buzz around him more thickly, instead of unresponsive Bill. He looked far more the type.

Grace Henson, she was that stoutish, flaxen-haired girl over there, waiting for the punch cup. Or was she? No, she was the less stout but still flaxen-haired one at the piano, softly playing for her own entertainment, no one near her. One wore glasses and one didn't. They must be sisters; there was too close a resemblance. It was the first time either one of them had been to the house.

She moved over to the piano and stood beside her. She might actually be enjoying doing that, for all Patrice knew, but she should at least have somebody taking an appreciative interest.

The girl at the keyboard smiled at her. "Now this." She was an accomplished player, keeping the music subdued, like an undertone to the conversations going on all over the room.

But suddenly all the nearby ones had stopped. The music went on alone for a note or two, sounding that much clearer than it had before.

The second flaxen-haired girl quitted her companion for a moment, stepped up behind the player's back, touched her just once on the shoulder, as if in some kind of esoteric remonstrance or reminder. That was all she did. Then she went right back to where she'd been sitting. The whole little pantomime had been so deft and quick it was hardly noticeable at all.

The player had broken off, uncertainly. She apparently had understood the message of the tap, but not its meaning. The slightly bewildered shrug she gave Patrice was evidence of that.

"Oh, finish it," Patrice protested unguardedly. "It was lovely. What's it called? I don't think I've ever heard it before."

"It's the Barcarolle, from *Tales of Hoffman*," the other girl answered unassumingly.

The answer itself was in anticlimax. Standing there beside the player, she became conscious of the congealing silence immediately about her, and knew it wasn't due to that, but to something that must have been said just before. It had already ended as she detected it, but awareness of it lingered on—in her. Something had happened just then.

I've said something wrong. I said something that was wrong just now. But I don't know what it was, and I don't know what to do about it.

She touched her punch cup to her lips; there was nothing else to do at the moment.

They only heard it near me. The music left my voice stranded, and that only made it all the more conspicuous. But who else in the room heard? Who else noticed? Maybe their faces will tell—

She turned slowly and glanced at them one by one, as if at random. Mother Hazzard was deep in conversation at the far end of the room, looking up over her chair at someone. She hadn't heard. The flaxen-haired girl who had delivered the cautioning tap had her back to her; she might have heard, and she might not. But if she had, it had made no impression; she was not aware of her. Guy Ennis was holding a lighter to a cigarette. He had to click it twice to make it spark, and it had all his attention. He didn't look up at her when her glance strayed lightly past his face. The two girls with Bill, they hadn't heard, it was easy to see that. They were oblivious of everything else but the bone of contention between them.

No one was looking at her. No one's eyes met hers.

Only Bill. His head was slightly down, and his forehead was querulously ridged, and he was gazing up from under his brows at her with a strange sort of inscrutability. Everything they were saying to him seemed to be going over his head. She couldn't tell if his thoughts were on her or a thousand miles away. But his eyes, at least, were.

She dropped her own.

And even after she did, she knew that his were still on her nonetheless.

As THEY climbed the stairs together, after, when everyone had gone, Mother Hazzard suddenly tightened an arm about her waist protectively.

"You were so brave about it," she said. "You did just the right thing, to pretend not to know what it was she was playing. Oh, but my dear, my heart went out to you, for a moment, when I saw you standing there. That look on your face. I wanted to run to you and put my arms around you. But I took my cue from you. I pretended not to notice anything either. She didn't mean anything by it. She's just a thoughtless little fool."

Patrice moved slowly up the stairs at her side, didn't answer.

"But at the sound of the very first notes," Mother Hazzard went on ruefully, "he seemed to be right back there in the room with all of us again. So *present*, you could almost see him in front of your eyes. The Barcarolle. His favorite song. He never sat down to a piano but what he played it. Whenever and wherever you heard that being played, you knew Hugh was about someplace."

"The Barcarolle," Patrice murmured almost inaudibly, as if speaking to herself. "His favorite song."

"—DIFFERENT now," Mother Hazzard was musing comfortably. "I was there once, as a girl, you know. Oh, many years ago. Tell me, has it changed much since those days?"

Suddenly she was looking directly at Patrice, in innocent exclusive inquiry.

"How can she answer that, Mother?" Father Hazzard cut in dryly. "She wasn't there when you were, so how would she know what it was like then?"

"Oh, you know what I mean," Mother Hazzard retorted indulgently. "Don't be so hanged precise."

"I suppose it has," Patrice answered feebly, turning the handle of her cup a little further toward her, as if about to lift it, and then not lifting it after all.

"You and Hugh were married there, weren't you, dear?" was the next desultory remark.

Again Father Hazzard interrupted before she could answer, this time with catastrophic rebuttal. "They were married in London, I thought. Don't you remember that letter he sent us at the time? I can still recall it: 'Married here yesterday.' London letterhead."

"Paris," said Mother Hazzard firmly. "Wasn't it, dear? I still have it upstairs. I can get it and show you. It has a Paris postmark." Then she tossed her head at him arbitrarily. "Anyway, this is one question Patrice *can* answer for herself."

There was suddenly a sickening chasm yawning at her feet, where a moment before all had been security of footing, and she couldn't turn back, yet she didn't know how to get across.

She could feel their three pairs of eyes on her. Bill's were raised now too, waiting in trustful expectancy that in a moment, with the wrong answer, would change to something else.

"London," she said softly, touching the handle of her cup as if deriving some sort of mystic clairvoyance from it. "But then we left immediately for Paris, on our honeymoon. I think what happened was, he began the letter in London, didn't have time to finish it, and then posted it from Paris."

"You see," said Mother Hazzard pertly, "I was partly right, anyhow."

"Now isn't that just like a woman," Father Hazzard marveled to his son.

Bill's eyes had remained on Patrice. There was something almost akin to grudging admiration in them, or did she imagine that?

"Excuse me," she said stifledly, thrusting her chair back. "I think I hear the baby crying."

AND then, a few weeks later, another pitfall. Or rather the same one, ever present, ever lurking treacherously underfoot as she walked this path of her own choosing.

It had been raining, and it grew heavily misted out. A rare occurrence for Caulfield. They were all there in the room with her, and she stopped by the window a moment in passing to glance out.

"Heavens," she exclaimed incautiously. "I haven't seen everything look so blurry since I was a child in San Fran. We used to get those fogs th—"

In the reflection on the lighted pane she saw Mother Hazzard's head go up, and knew before she had even turned back to face them she had said the wrong thing. Trodden incautiously again, where there was no support.

"In San Francisco, dear?" Mother Hazzard's voice was guilelessly puzzled. "But I thought you were raised in— Hugh wrote us you were originally from—" And then she didn't finish it, withholding the clue; no helpful second choice was forthcoming this time. Instead, a flat question followed. "Is that where you were born, dear?"

"No," Patrice said distinctly, and knew what the next question was sure to be. A question she could not have answered at the moment.

Bill raised his head suddenly, turned it inquiringly toward the stairs. "I think I hear the youngster crying, Patrice."

"I'll go up and take a look," she said gratefully, and left the room.

He was in a soundless sleep when she got to him. He wasn't making a whimper that anyone could possibly have heard. She stood there by him with a look of thoughtful scrutiny on her face.

Had he really thought he heard the baby crying?

21

THEN there was the day she was slowly sauntering along Congress Avenue, window-shopping. Congress Avenue was the main retail thoroughfare. Looking at this window display, looking at that, not intending to buy anything, not needing to. But enjoying herself all the more in this untrammeled state. Enjoying the crowd of well-dressed shoppers thronging the sunlit sidewalk all about her, the great majority of them women at that forenoon hour of the day. Enjoying the bustle, the spruce activity, they conveyed. Enjoying this carefree moment, this brief respite (an errand for Mother Hazzard, a promise to pick something up for her, was what had brought her downtown), all the more for knowing that it was a legitimate absence, not a dereliction, and that the baby was safe, well taken care of while she was gone. And that she'd enjoy returning to it all the more, after this short diversion.

It was simply a matter of taking the bus at the next stop ahead, instead of at the nearer one behind her, and strolling the difference between the two.

And then from somewhere behind her she heard her name called. She recognized the voice at the first syllable. Cheerful, sunny. Bill. She had her smile of greeting ready before she had even turned her head.

Two of his long, energetic strides and he was beside her.

"Hello there. I thought I recognized you."

They stopped for a minute, face to face.

"What are you doing out of the office?"

"I was on my way back just now. Had to go over and see a man. And you?"

"I came down to get Mother some imported English yarn she had waiting for her at Bloom's. Before they send it out, I can be there and back with it."

"I'll walk with you," he offered. "Good excuse to loaf. As far as the next corner anyhow."

"That's where I'm taking my bus anyway," she told him.

They turned and resumed their course, but at the snail's pace she had been maintaining by herself before now.

He crinkled his nose and squinted upward appreciatively. "It does a fellow good to get out in the sun once in a while."

"Poor abused man. I'd like to have a penny for every time you're out of that office during hours."

He chuckled unabashedly. "Can I help it if Dad sends me? Of course, I always happen to get right in front of him when he's looking around for someone to do the legwork."

They stopped.

"Those're nice," she said appraisingly.

"Yes," he agreed. "But what are they?"

"You know darned well they're hats. Don't try to be so superior."

They went on, stopped again.

"Is this what they call window-shopping?"

"This is what they call window-shopping. As if you didn't know."

"It's fun. You don't get anywhere. But you see a lot."

"You may like it now, because it's a novelty. Wait'll you're married and get a lot of it. You won't like it then."

The next window display was an offering of fountain pens, a narrow little showcase not more than two or three yards in width.

She didn't offer to stop there. It was now he who did, halting her with him as a result.

"Wait a minute. That reminds me. I need a new pen. Will you come in with me a minute and help me pick one out?"

"I ought to be getting back," she said halfheartedly.

"It'll only take a minute. I'm a quick buyer."

"I don't know anything about pens," she demurred.

"I don't myself. That's just it. Two heads are better than one." He'd taken her lightly by the arm by now, to try to induce her. "Ah, come on. I'm the sort they sell anything to when I'm alone."

"I don't believe a word of it. You just want company." She laughed, but she went inside with him nevertheless.

He offered her a chair facing the counter. A case of pens was brought out and opened. They were discussed between him and the salesman, she taking no active part. Several were uncapped, filled at a waiting bottle of ink at hand on the counter, and tried out on a pad of scratch paper, also at hand for that purpose.

She looked on, trying to show an interest she did not really feel.

Suddenly he said to her, "How do you like the way this writes?" and thrust one of them between her fingers and the block of paper under her hand, before she quite knew what had happened.

Incautiously, her mind on the proportions and weight of the barrel in her grasp, her attention fixed on what sort of a track the nib would leave, whether a broad bold one or a thin wiry one, she put it to the pad. Suddenly "Helen" stood there on the topmost leaf, almost as if produced by automatic writing. Or rather, in the fullest sense of the word, it was just that. She checked herself just in time to prevent the second name from flowing out of the pen. It was already on the preliminary upward stroke of a capital G, when she jerked it clear.

"Here, let me try it a minute myself." Without warning he'd taken both pen and pad back again, before she could do anything to obliterate or alter what was on it.

Whether he saw it or not, she couldn't tell. He gave no indication. Yet it was right there under his eyes, he must have, how could he have failed to?

He drew a cursory line or two, desisted.

"No," he said to the salesman. "Let me see that one."

While he was reaching into the case, she managed to deftly peel off the topmost leaf with that damaging "Helen" on it. Crumpled it surreptitiously in her hand, dropped it to the floor.

And then, belatedly, realized that perhaps this was even worse than had she left it on there where it was. For surely he'd seen it anyway, and now she'd only pointed up the fact that she did not want him to. In other words, she'd doubly damned herself; first by the error, then by taking such pains to try to efface it.

Meanwhile, his interest in the matter of pens had all at once flagged. He looked at the clerk, about to speak, and she could have almost predicted what he was about to say—had he said it—his expression conveyed it so well. "Never mind. I'll stop in again some other time." But then instead he gave her a look, and as though recalled to the necessity for maintaining some sort of plausibility, said hurriedly, almost indifferently, "All right, here, make it this one. Send it over to my office later on."

He scarcely looked at it. It didn't seem to matter to him which one he took.

And, she reminded herself, after making such to-do about her coming in with him to help him select one.

"Shall we go?" he said, a trifle reticently.

Their parting was strained. She didn't know whether it was due to him or due to herself. Or just due to her own imagining. But it seemed to her to lack the jaunty spontaneity of their meeting just a few minutes ago.

He didn't thank her for helping him select a pen, and she was grateful for that at least. But his eyes were suddenly remote, abstracted, where until now they had been wholly on her at every turn of speech. They seemed to be looking up this way toward the top of a building, looking down that way toward the far end of the street, looking everywhere but at her anymore, even while he was saying, "Here's your bus," and arming her into it, and reaching in from where he stood to pay the driver her fare. "Good-bye. Get home all right. See you tonight." And tipped his hat, and seemed to have already forgotten her even before he had completed the act of turning away and going about his business.

And yet somehow she knew that just the reverse was true. That he was more conscious of her than ever, now that he seemed least so. Distance had intervened between them, that was all.

She looked down at her lap, while the bus swept her along past the crowded sidewalks. Funny how quickly a scene could change, the same scene; the sunlit pavements and the bustling shoppers weren't fun anymore to watch.

If it had been a premeditated test, a trap— But no, it couldn't have been that. That much at least she was sure of, though it was no satisfaction. He *couldn't* have known that he was going to run into her just where he had, that they were going to walk along just as they had, toward that pen emporium. At the time he'd left the house this morning, she hadn't even known herself that she was coming downtown like this; that had come up later. So he couldn't have lain in wait for her there, to accost her. That much at least had been spontaneous, purely accidental.

But maybe as they were strolling along, and he first looked up and saw the store sign, that was when it had occurred to him, and he'd improvised it, on the spur of the moment. What was commonly said must have occurred to him then, as it only occurred to her now. That when people try out a new pen, they invariably write their real names. It's almost compulsory.

And yet, even for such an undeliberated, on-the-spot test as that, there must have been some formless suspicion of her already latent in his mind, in one way or another, or it wouldn't have suggested itself to him.

Little fool, she said to herself bitterly as she tugged at the overhead cord and prepared to alight, why didn't you think of that before you went in there with him? What good was hindsight now?

A night or two later his discarded coat was slung over a chair, and he wasn't in the room with it at the moment. She needed a pencil for something for a moment anyhow, that was her excuse for it. She sought the pocket and took out the fountain pen she found clasped to it. It was gold and had his initials engraved on it; some valued, long-used birthday or Christmas present from one of his parents probably. Moreover, it was in perfect writing order, couldn't have been improved on, left a clear, deep, rich trace. And he wasn't the sort of man who went around displaying two fountain pens at a time.

It had been a test, all right. And she had given a positive reaction, as positive as he could have hoped for.

22

SHE'D heard the doorbell ring some time before, and dim sounds of conglomerate greeting follow it in the hall below, and knew by that some visitor must have arrived, and must still be down there. She didn't think anymore about it. She'd had Hughie in his little portable tub at the moment, and that, while it was going on, was a full-time job for anyone's attention. By the time she'd finished drying and talcuming and dressing him, putting him to bed for the night, and then lingering treacherously by him a while longer, to watch her opportunity and worm the last celluloid bath duck out of his tightly closed little fist, the better part of an hour had gone by. She felt sure the caller, whoever he was, must already be long gone by that time. That it had been a masculine visitor was something she could take for granted; anyone feminine from six to sixty would automatically have been ushered upstairs by the idolatrous Mother Hazzard to look in on the festive rite of her grandson's bath. In fact it was the first time she herself had missed attending one in weeks, if only to hold the towel, prattle in an unintelligible gibberish with the small person in the tub, and generally get in the uncomplaining mother's way. Only something of importance could have kept her away.

She thought they were being unusually quiet below, when she finally came out of her room and started down the stairs. There was a single, droning, low-pitched voice going on, as if somebody were reading aloud, and no one else was audible.

They were all in the library, she discovered a moment later; a room that was never used much in the evenings. And when it was, never by all of them together, at one time. She could see them in there twice over, the first time from the stairs themselves, as she came down them, and then in an after-glimpse, through the open doorway at nearer range, as she doubled back around the foot of the stairs and passed by in the hall just outside.

The three of them were in there, and there was a man with them whom she didn't know, although she realized she must have seen him at least one or more times before, as she had everyone who came to this house. He was at the table, the reading lamp lit, droning aloud in a monotonous, singsong voice. It wasn't a book; it seemed more like a typed report. Every few moments a brittly crackling sheet would sweep back in reverse and go under the others.

No one else was saying a word. They were sitting at varying

distances and at varying degrees of attention. Father Hazzard was drawn up to the table with the monologist, following every word closely and nodding in benign accord from time to time. Mother Hazzard was in an easy chair, a basket on her lap, darning something and only occasionally looking up in sketchy aural participation. And Bill, strangely present, was off on the very outskirts of the conclave, a leg dangling over the arm of his chair, head tilted all the way back with a protruding pipe thrust ceilingward, and giving very little indication of listening at all. His eyes had a look of vacancy, as though his mind were elsewhere while his body was dutifully and filially in the room with them.

She tried to get by without being seen, but Mother Hazzard looked up at just the wrong time and caught the flicker of her figure past the door gap. "There she is now," she said. A moment later her retarding call had overtaken and halted her. "Patrice, come in here a moment, dear. We want you."

She turned and went back, with a sudden constriction in her throat.

The droning voice had interrupted itself to wait. A private investigator? No, no, he couldn't be. She'd met him here in the house on a friendly basis, she was sure of it. But those voluminous briefs littered in front of him—

"Patrice, you know Ty Winthrop."

"Yes, I know we've met before." She went over and shook hands with him. She kept her eyes carefully off the table. And it wasn't easy.

"Ty is Father's lawyer," Mother Hazzard said indulgently. As though that were really no way to describe an old friend, but it was the shortest one for present purposes.

"And golf rival," supplied the man at the table.

"Rival?" Father Hazzard snorted disgustedly. "I don't call that rivalry, what you put up. A rival has to come up somewhere near you. Charity tournament is more what I'd call it."

Bill's head and pipe had come down to the horizontal again. "Lick him with one hand tied behind your back, eh, Dad?" he egged him on.

"Yeah, *my* hand," snapped the lawyer, with a private wink for the son. "Especially last Sunday."

"Now, you three," reproved Mother Hazzard beamingly. "I have things to do. And so has Patrice. I can't sit in here all night."

They became serious again. Bill had risen and drawn up a chair beside the table for her. "Sit down, Patrice, and join the party," he invited.

"Yes, we want you to hear this, Patrice," Father Hazzard urged as she hesitated. "It concerns you."

Her hand tried to stray betrayingly toward her throat. She kept it down by sheer willpower. She seated herself, a little uneasily.

The lawyer cleared his throat. "Well, I think that about takes care of it, Donald. The rest of it remains as it was before."

Father Hazzard hitched his chair nearer. "All right. Ready for me to sign now?"

Mother Hazzard bit off a thread with her teeth, having come to the end of something or other. She began to put things away in her basket, preparatory to departure. "You'd better tell Patrice what it is first, dear. Don't you want her to know?"

"I'll tell her for you," Winthrop offered. "I can put it in fewer words than you." He turned toward her and gazed friendlily over the tops of his reading glasses. "Donald's changing the provisions of his will, by adding a codicil. You see, in the original, after Grace here was provided for, there was an equal division of the residue made between Bill and Hugh. Well, now we're altering that to make it one-quarter of the residue to Bill and the remainder to you."

She could feel her face beginning to flame, as though a burning crimson light were focused on it, and it alone, that they could all see. An agonizing sensation of wanting to push away from the table and make her escape, and of being held trapped there in her chair, came over her.

She tried to speak quietly, quelling her voice by moistening her lips twice over. "I don't want you to do that. I don't want to be included."

"Don't look that way about it," Bill said with a genial laugh. "You're not doing anybody out of anything. I have Dad's business—"

"It was Bill's own suggestion," Mother Hazzard let her know.

"I gave both the boys a lump sum in cash, to start them off, on the day they each reached their twenty-first—"

She was on her feet now, facing all of them in turn, almost panic-stricken. "No, please! Don't put my name down on it at all! I don't want my name to go down on it!" She all but wrung her clasped hands toward Father Hazzard. "Dad! Won't you listen to me?"

"It's on account of Hugh, dear," Mother Hazzard let him know in a tactful aside. "Can't you understand?"

"Well, I know; we all feel bad about Hugh. But she has to go on living just the same. She has a child to think of. And these things shouldn't be postponed on account of sentiment; they have to be taken care of at the right time."

She turned and fled from the room. They made no attempt to follow her.

She closed the door after her. She stormed back and forth, two, three times, holding her head locked in her upended arms. "Swindler!" burst from her muffledly. "Thief! It's just like someone climbing in through a window and—"

There was a low knock at the door about half an hour later. She went over and opened it, and Bill was standing there.

"Hello," he said diffidently.

"Hello," she said with equal diffidence.

It was as though they hadn't seen one another for two or three days past, instead of just half an hour before.

"He signed it," he said. "After you went up. Winthrop took it back with him. Witnessed and all. It's done now, whether you wanted it or not."

She didn't answer. The battle had been lost, downstairs, before, and this was just the final communiqué.

He was looking at her in a way she couldn't identify. It seemed to have equal parts of shrewd appraisal and blank incomprehension in it, and there was just a dash of admiration added.

"You know," he said, "I don't know why you acted like that about it. And I don't agree with you. I think you were wrong in acting like that about it." He lowered his voice a little in confidence. "But somehow or other I'm glad you acted like that about it. I like you better for acting like that about it." He shoved his hand out to her suddenly. "Want to shake good night?"

23

SHE was alone in the house. That is, alone just with Hughie, in his crib upstairs, and Aunt Josie, in her room all the way at the back. They'd gone out to visit the Michaelsons, old friends.

It was nice to be alone in the house once in a while. Not too often, not all the time; that would have run over into loneliness. And she'd known what that was once, only too well, and didn't want to ever again.

But it was nice to be alone like this, alone *without* loneliness, just for an hour or two, just from nine until eleven, with the sure knowledge that they were coming back soon. With the whole house her own to roam about in; upstairs, down, into this room, into that. Not that she couldn't at other times—but this had a special feeling to it, doing it when no one else was about. It did something to her. It nourished her feeling of *belonging*, replenished it.

They'd asked her if she didn't want to come with them, but she'd begged off. Perhaps because she knew that if she stayed home alone, she'd get this very feeling from it.

They didn't importune her. They never importuned, never repeated any invitation to the point of weariness. They respected you as an individual, she reflected; that was one of the nice things about them. Only one of the nice; there were so many others.

"Then next time, maybe." Mother had smiled in parting, from the door.

"Next time without fail," she promised. "They're very nice people."

She roamed about for a while first, getting her "feel" of the place, saturating herself in that blessed sensation of "belonging." Touching a chair-back here, fingering the texture of a window drape there.

Mine. My house. My parents' house and mine. Mine. Mine. My *home*. My chair. My window drape. No, hang back like that, that's the way I want you to.

Silly? Childish? Fanciful? No doubt. But who is without childishness, fancies? What is life without them? Or, *is* there life without them?

She went into Aunt Josie's pantry, took the lid off the cookie jar, took one out, took a big bite out of it.

She wasn't hungry. They'd all finished a big dinner only a couple of hours ago. But—

My house. I can do this. I'm entitled to them. They're waiting there for me, to help myself whenever I feel like it.

She put the lid on the jar, started to put the light out.

She changed her mind suddenly, went back, took out a second one.

My house. I can even take two if I want to. Well, I *will* take two.

And one in each hand, each with a big defiant bite taken out of it, she came out of there. They weren't food for the mouth, actually; they were food for the soul.

The last crumbs brushed off her fingers, she decided to read a book finally. Utter repose had come to her now, a sense of peace and well-being that was almost therapeutic in its depth. It was a sensation of *healing*; of becoming one, becoming whole again. As though the last vestiges of an old ache, from an old split in her personality (as indeed there was one in the fullest sense), had been effaced. A psychiatrist could have written a learned paper on this; that just roaming about a house, in utter security, in utter relaxation, for half an hour or so, could achieve such a result for her, beyond all capacity of cold-blooded science, in the clinic, to have done likewise. But human beings are human beings, and science isn't what they need; it's a home, a house of their own, that no one can take away from them.

It was the right time, almost the only time, for reading a book. You could give it your full attention, you could lose yourself in it. You became one with it for a while, selfless.

In the library, it took her some time to make a definitive selection. She did a considerable amount of leaf-fluttering along the shelves, made two false starts back to the chair for an opening paragraph or two, before she'd finally settled on something that gave an indication of suiting her.

Marie Antoinette, by Katharine Anthony.

She'd never cared much for fiction, somehow. Something about it made her slightly uncomfortable, perhaps a reminder of the drama in her own life. She liked things (her mind expressed it) *that had really happened.* Really happened, but long ago and far away, to someone entirely else, someone that never could be confused with herself. In the case of a fictional character, you soon, involuntarily, began identifying yourself with him or her. In the case of a character who had once been an actual living personage, you did not. You sympathized objectively, but it ended there. It was always, from first to last, someone else. Because it had once, in reality, *been* someone else. (Escape, they would have called this, though in her case it was the reverse of what it was for others. They escaped from humdrum reality into fictional drama. She escaped from too much personal drama into a reality of the past.)

For an hour, maybe more, she was one with a woman dead a hundred and fifty years; she lost track of time.

Dimly, with only a marginal part of her faculties, she heard brakes go on somewhere outside in the quiet night.

". . . Axel Fersen drove swiftly through the dark streets." (They're back. I'll finish this chapter first.) "An hour and a half later, the coach passed through the gate of Saint-Martin. . . ."

A key turned in the front door. It opened, then it closed. But no murmur of homecoming voices eddied in. Vocal silence, if not the total kind. Firm, energetic footsteps, a single pair, struck across the preliminary gap of bare flooring adjacent to the door, then blurred off along the hall carpeting.

". . . A little way beyond, they saw a large traveling-carriage drawn up at the side of the road." (No, that's Bill, not they. He's the one just came in. I forgot, they didn't take the car with them. The Michaelsons live just around the corner.) ". . . a large traveling-carriage drawn up at the side of the road. . . ."

The tread went to the back. Aunt Josie's pantry light flashed on again. She couldn't have seen it from where she was, but she knew it by the click of its switch. She knew all the lights by the clicks of their switches. The direction from which the click came, and its sharpness or faintness of tone. You can learn those things about a house.

She heard water surge from a tap, and then an emptied glass go down. Then the lid of the cookie jar went down, with its heavy, hollowed, ringing, porcelain thud. It stayed down for some time, too, was in no hurry to go back on again.

". . . drawn up at the side of the road." (Aunt Josie'll have a fit. She always scolds him. She never scolds me, for doing the very same thing. I guess she used to when he was a boy, and can't get over the habit.) "The pseudo Madame Korff and her party entered the carriage. . . ."

The lid went back on again at long last. The footsteps started forward again, emerged into the back of the hall. They stopped short, backed up a step; the floor creaked slightly with doubled weight in one place.

". . ." (He dropped a chunk on the floor, stopped to pick it up. Doesn't want her to see it lying there in the morning and know what he's been up to. I bet he's still afraid of Aunt Josie in his heart, in a little-boy way.) ". . ."

But her thoughts were not consciously of him or on him. They were on her book. It was the perimeter of her mind, the unused residue, that kept up a running commentary to itself, and which the center of her attention paid no heed to.

He subsided for a while, was lost to awareness. Must have been slumped somewhere, finishing his cookies. Probably with a leg thrown over a chair arm, if he was in a chair at all.

He had known they were going over to the Michaelsons, and

must have thought she had gone with them, that he was alone in the house. The library was to the right of the stairs, and he had taken the left channel, to the pantry and returned, hadn't come near here as yet, so he couldn't have known that she was in here. The shaded lamp she was beside had a limited radius of reflection that did not reach past the room doorway.

Suddenly his lithe footfalls were under way again, had recommenced, the nibbling interlude at an end. They struck out into the hall again, clarifying as they emerged from wherever it was he had been, rounded the bottom of the stairs, and turned in on this side. They were coming straight toward here, toward this room she was unsuspectedly in.

She went ahead steadily reading, trapped by the mounting interest of the passage she had just entered upon, held fast. Didn't even raise her eyes.

His tread reached the threshold. Then it stopped short there, almost with a recoil.

For perhaps a moment he stood stock-still, looking at her.

Then, abruptly, he took an awkward step in retreat, a full step to the rear, turned, went away again.

It was almost subconsciously that she knew all this; not in full consciousness, at least not as yet. It was there, clinging to her awareness, but it hadn't penetrated it as yet.

". . ." (Why did he turn and go away like that, when he saw me in here alone?) ". . . and disposed themselves upon the comfortable cushions. . . ." (He intended coming in here. He did come as far as the door. Then when he saw that I was in here, and didn't seem to have seen him yet, he backed away. Why? Why was that?) "Axel Fersen took the reins. . . ."

Slowly the spell of the book unraveled, disintegrated. Her eyes left its pages for the first time. She raised her head questioningly, still holding the book open before her.

Why? Why did he do that?

It isn't that he was afraid of disturbing me. We're all one family; we don't stand on ceremony like that with one another. We all go from room to room as we like without a by-your-leave, except in the upstairs rooms, and this isn't upstairs, this is down here. He didn't even say hello. When he saw that I didn't see him, he wanted it left that way, did his best to keep it that way, tried not to attract my attention. Withdrew *backward* the first step, and only then turned around.

The front door had reopened, but without closing behind him. He'd gone out front for a moment, to put the car away. She heard the thump of its door as he shut it on himself, heard its gears mesh into motion.

Doesn't he like me? Is that why he doesn't want to find himself alone in a room with me, when no one else is here? Is he holding something against me? I thought—it seemed—as if his full confidence had been given to me long ago, but— To balk like that, curb himself, almost swerve away, at the very threshold.

And then suddenly, quite simply, almost matter-of-factly, she knew. It came to her. Some indefinable something had told her. Something that no word could explain. Something too tenuous to bear the weight of *any* words.

No, it's not because he doesn't like me. It's because he does like me, *does* like me, that he backed away like that, doesn't want to be in the room alone with me if he can avoid it. Likes me too well. Is already beginning to fall in love with me. And—and thinks he shouldn't. Is fighting it. That hopeless, last-ditch fight that's never won.

Determinedly, but quite unhurriedly, she closed her book, carried it over to the gap from which she'd extracted it, pushed it in. She left the lamp on for him (since he had seemed to want to come in here), but quitted the room herself, left it to him, went out into the hall, went up the stairs and into her own room, closed the door of that for the night.

She undid her hair, brushed it for retiring.

She heard the rumble of the garage doors, heard the padlock strike against them as he let it fall back to rest, heard him come into the house again. He went straight back toward the library, and went in, this time unhesitatingly (to accost her now, to face it, to bring it out, his decision taken during those few minutes' breathing spell?)—to find it empty. The lamp on, the reader gone.

Seconds later she remembered that she'd left her cigarette burning there, on the table, under the lamp, beside where she'd been sitting. Had forgotten to pick it up when she came out. It must be burning still; she'd only just lit it before she'd first heard the car drive up outside.

It wasn't that she was alarmed about possible damage. He'd see it at a glance and put it out for her.

But it would tell him. For, just as he had intended coming in when he hadn't, it would reveal to him that she *hadn't* intended getting up and leaving when she had.

She not only knew, now, that he was beginning to love her, but, by token of that telltale cigarette, he knew that she knew.

IN THE light of the full-bodied moon the flower garden at the back of the house was as bright as noon when she stepped out into it. The sanded paths that ran around it foursquare, and through it like an X, gleamed like snow, and her shadow glided along them azure against their whiteness. The little rock pool in the center was polka-dotted with silver disks, and the wafers coalesced and separated again as if in motion, though they weren't, as her point of perspective continually shifted with her rotary stroll.

The perfume of the rosebushes was heavy on the June night, and sleepy little insects made a somnolent humming noise, as though they were talking in their sleep.

She hadn't wanted to sleep yet, and she hadn't wanted to read; it was too close in the library with the lamp on. She hadn't wanted to sit alone on the front porch any longer, once Mother and Father Hazzard had left her and gone up to their room. She'd gone up a moment and looked in at Hughie, to see if he was all right, and then she'd come out here. To the flower garden in the back, safely secluded behind its tall surrounding hedge.

Eleven struck melodiously from the little Reformed church over on Beechwood Drive, and the echoes lingered in the still air, filling her with a sense of peace and well-being.

A quiet voice, seeming to come from just over her shoulder, said, "Hello; I thought that was you down there, Patrice."

She turned, startled, and couldn't locate him for a minute. He was above her, perched edgewise on the sill of his open window.

"Mind if I come down and join you for a cigarette?"

"I'm going in now," she said hastily, but he'd already disappeared.

He stepped down from the back porch, and the moonlight sifted over his head and shoulders like talcum as he came toward her. She turned in company with him, and they walked slowly on together side by side. Once all around the outside path, and then once through a bisecting middle one.

She reached out and touched a flower once in passing; bent it a little toward her, then let it sway back again undamaged. A full-blown white rose; the perfume was almost like a bombshell in their faces for a moment.

He didn't even do that much, didn't do anything. Didn't say anything. Just walked beside her. One hand slung in his pocket. Looking steadily down, as though the sight of the path fascinated him.

"I hate to tear myself away, it's so lovely down here," she said at last.

"I don't give a hang about gardens," he answered almost gruffly. "Nor walking in them. Nor the flowers in them. You know why I came down here. Do I have to tell you?"

He flung his cigarette down violently, backhand, with the same gesture as if something had angered him.

Suddenly she was acutely frightened. She'd stopped short.

"No, wait, Bill. Bill, wait— Don't—"

"Don't what? I haven't said anything yet. But you know already, don't you? I'm sorry, Patrice, I've got to tell you. You've got to listen. It's got to come out."

She was holding out her hand protestingly toward him, as if trying to ward off something. She took a backward step away, broke their proximity.

"*I* don't like it," he said rebelliously. "It does things to me that are new. I was never bothered before. I never even had the sweetheart-crushes that they all do. I guess that was my way to be. But this is it, Patrice. This is it now, all right."

"No, wait— Not now. Not yet. This isn't the time—"

"This is the time, and this is the night, and this is the place. There'll never be another night like this, not if we both live to be a hundred. Patrice, I love you, and I want you to ma—"

"Bill!" she pleaded, terrified.

"Now you've heard it, and now you're running away. Patrice," he asked forlornly, "what's so terrible about it?"

She'd gained the lower-porch step, was poised on it for a moment in arrested flight. He came after her slowly, in a sort of acquiescent frustration, rather than in importunate haste.

"I'm no lover," he said. "I can't say it right—"

"Bill," she said again, almost grief-strickenly.

"Patrice, I see you every day and—" He flung his arms apart helplessly. "What am I to do? I didn't ask for it. I think it's something good. I think it's something that should be."

She leaned her head for a moment against the porch post, as if in distress. "Why did you have to say it yet? Why couldn't you have— Give me more time. Please, give me more time. Just a few months—"

"Do you want me to take it back, Patrice?" he asked ruefully. "How can I now? How could I, even if I hadn't spoken? Patrice, it's so long since, now. Is it Hugh, is it still Hugh?"

"I've never been in love bef—" she started to say penitently. She stopped suddenly.

He looked at her strangely.

I've said too much, flashed through her mind. Too much, or not enough. And then in sorrowful confirmation: Not enough by far.

"I'm going in now." The shadow of the porch dropped between them like an indigo curtain.

He didn't try to follow. He stood there where she'd left him.

"You're afraid I'll kiss you."

"No, that isn't what I'm afraid of," she murmured almost inaudibly. "I'm afraid I'll want you to."

The door closed after her.

He stood out there in the full bleach of the moonlight, motionless, looking sadly downward.

25

In the morning the world was sweet just to look at from her window. The sense of peace, of safety, of belonging, was being woven about her stronger all the time. Soon nothing could tear its fabric apart again. To wake up in your own room, in your own home, your own roof over your head. To find your little son awake before you and peering expectantly out through his crib, and giving you that crowing smile of delight that was already something special he gave to no one but you. To lift him up and hold him to you, and have to curb yourself, you wanted to squeeze so tightly. Then to carry him over to the window with you, and hold the curtain back, and look out at the world.

Show him the world you'd found for him, the world you'd made for him.

The early sunlight like goldenrod pollen lightly dusting the sidewalks and the roadway out front. The azure shadows under the trees and at the lee sides of all the houses. A man sprinkling a lawn a few doors down, the water fraying from the nozzle of his hose twinkling like diamonds. He looked up and saw you, and he gave you a neighborly wave of the hand, though you didn't know him very well. And you took Hughie's little hand at the wrist and waved it back to him in answering greeting.

Yes, in the mornings the world was sweet all right.

Then to dress, to dress for two, and to go downstairs to the pleasant room waiting for you below; to Mother Hazzard, and her fresh-picked flowers, and her affectionate, sunny greeting, and the mirror-like reflection of the coffee percolator (that always delighted him so) showing squat, pudgy images seated around it on its various facets: an elderly lady, and a much younger lady, and a very young young-man, the center of attraction in his high chair.

To be safe, to be at home, to be among your own.

Even mail for you, a letter of your own, waiting for you at your place. She felt a pleased little sense of completion at sight of it. There was no greater token of permanency, of belonging, than that. Mail of your own, sent to your home.

"Mrs. Patrice Hazzard," and the address. Once that name had frightened her. It didn't now. In a little while she would no longer even remember that there had been another name, once, before it. A lonely, frightened name, drifting ownerless, unclaimed, about the world now—

"Now Hughie, not so fast, finish what you've got first."

She opened it, and there was nothing in it. Or rather, nothing written on it. For a moment she thought there must have been a mistake. Just blank paper. No, wait, the other way around—

Three small words, almost buried in the seam that folded the sheet in two, almost overlooked in the snowy expanse that surrounded them.

Who are you?

26

IN THE mornings the world was bittersweet to look at from her window. To wake up in a room that wasn't rightfully yours. That you knew—and you knew somebody else knew—you had no right to be in. The early sunlight was pale and bleak upon the ground, and under all the trees and on the lee side of all the houses, tatters of night lingered, diluted to blue but still gloomy and forbidding. A man sprinkling the lawn a few doors down was a stranger; a stranger you knew by sight. He looked up, and you hurriedly shrank back from the window, child and all, lest he see you. Then a moment later, you already wished you hadn't done that, but it was too late, it was done.

Was he the one? Was he?

It isn't as much fun anymore to dress for two. And when you start down the stairs with Hughie, those stairs you've come down so many hundreds of times, now at last you've learned what it's like to come down them heavyhearted and troubled, as you said you might someday have to, that very first night of all. For that's how you're coming down them now.

Mother Hazzard at the table, beaming; and the flowers; and the gargoyle-like reflections on the percolator panels. But you only have eyes for one thing, furtive, straining eyes, from as far back as the threshold of the doorway. From farther back than that, even; from the first moment the table has come into sight. Is there any white on it, over on your side of it? Is there any rectangular white patch showing there, by or near your place? It's easy to tell, for the cloth has a printed pattern, with dabs of red and green.

"Patrice, didn't you sleep well, dear?" Mother Hazzard asked solicitously. "You look a little peaked."

She hadn't looked peaked out on the stairs a moment ago. She'd only been heavyhearted and troubled then.

She settled Hughie in his chair and took a little longer than was necessary. Keep your eyes away from it. Don't look at it. Don't think about it. Don't try to find out what's in it, you don't want to know what's in it. Let it stay there until after the meal, then tear it up un—

"Patrice, you're spilling it on his chin. Here, let me."

She had nothing to do with her own hands, from that point on. And she felt as though she had so many of them; four or five at least. She reached for the coffeepot, and a corner of it was in the way. She reached for the sugar bowl, and another corner of it was in the way. She drew her napkin toward her, and it sidled two or three inches nearer her, riding on that. It was all about her, it was everywhere at once!

She wanted to scream, and she clenched her hand tightly, down beside her chair. I mustn't do that, I mustn't. Hughie's right here next to me, and Mother's just across the table—

Open it, open it fast. Quick, while you still have the courage.

The paper made a shredding sound, her finger was so thick and maladroit.

One word more this time.

Where are you from?

She clenched her hand again, down low beside her chair. White dissolved into it, disappearing through the finger crevices.

27

IN THE mornings the world was bitter to look at from the window. To wake up in a strange room, in a strange house. To pick up your baby—that was the only thing that was rightfully yours—and edge toward the window with him, creeping up slantwise and peering from the far side of it, barely lifting the curtain; not stepping forward to the middle of it and throwing the curtain widely back. That was for people in their own homes, not for you. And out there, nothing. Nothing that belonged to you or was for you. The hostile houses of a hostile town. An icy wash of sun upon a stony ground. Dark shadows like frowns under each tree and leeward of each house. The man watering the lawn didn't turn around to greet you today. He was more than a stranger now; he was a potential enemy.

She carried her boy with her downstairs, and every step was like a knell. She was holding her eyes closed when she first went into the dining room. She couldn't help it; she couldn't bring herself to open them for a moment.

"Patrice, you don't look right to me at all. You ought to see your color against that child's."

She opened her eyes.

Nothing there.

But it would come. It would come again. It had come once, twice; it would come again. Tomorrow maybe. The day after. Or the day after that. It would surely come again. There was nothing to do but wait. To sit there, stricken, helpless, waiting. It was like holding your head bowed under a leaky faucet, waiting for the next icy drop to detach itself and fall.

In the mornings the world was bitter, and in the evenings it was full of shadows creeping formlessly about her, threatening from one moment to the next to close in and engulf her.

28

SHE hadn't slept well. That was the first thing she was conscious of on awakening. The cause, the reason for it, that came right with it. That was what really mattered; not the fact that she hadn't slept well, but knowing the cause, the reason for it. Only too well.

It wasn't new. It was occurring all the time lately, this not sleeping well. It was the rule rather than the exception.

The strain was beginning to tell on her. Her resistance was wearing away. Her nerves were slowly being drawn taut, a little more so each day. She was nearing a danger point, she knew. She couldn't stand very much more of it. It wasn't when they came; it was in-between, waiting for the next one to come. The longer it took to come, the greater her tension, instead of the less. It was like that well-known simile of the second dropped shoe, prolonged ad infinitum.

She couldn't stand much more of it. "If there's another one," she told herself, "something will snap. Don't let there be another one. Don't."

She looked at herself in the glass. Not through vanity, conceit, to see whether damage had been done her looks. To confirm, objectively, the toll that was being taken. Her face was pale and worn. It was growing thinner again, losing its roundness, growing back toward that gauntness of cheek it had had in New York. Her eyes were a little too shadowed underneath, and just a little too bright. She looked tired and frightened. Not acutely so, but chronically. And that was what was being done to her by this.

She dressed herself, and then Hughie, and carried him down with her. It was so pleasant in the dining room, in the early morning like this. The new-minted sun pouring in, the color of champagne; the crisp chintz curtains; the cheery colored ware on the table; the fragrant aroma of the coffeepot; the savory odor of fresh-made toast seeping through the napkin thrown over it to keep it warm. Mother Hazzard's flowers in the center of the table, always less than an hour old, picked from her garden at the back. Mother Hazzard herself, spruce and gay in her printed morning dress, beaming at her. Home. Peace.

"Leave me in peace," she pleaded inwardly. "Let me be. Let me have all this. Let me enjoy it, as it's meant to be enjoyed, as it's waiting around to be enjoyed. Don't take it from me. Let me keep it."

She went around the table to her and kissed her, and held Hughie out to her to be kissed. Then she settled him in his high chair, between the two of them, and sat down herself.

Then she saw them, waiting for her.

The one on top was a department-store sales brochure, sealed in an envelope. She could identify it by the letterhead in the upper corner. But there was something under it, another one. Its corners stuck out a little past the top one.

She was afraid to bring it into fuller view; she postponed it.

She spooned Hughie's cereal to his mouth, took alternating sips of her own fruit juice. It was poisoning the meal, it was tightening up her nerves.

It mightn't be one of those, it might be something else. Her hand moved with a jerk, and the department-store folder was out of the way.

Mrs. Patrice Hazzard

It was addressed in pen and ink, a personal letter. She never got letters like that from anyone; who wrote to her, whom did she know? It must be, it was, one of those again. She felt a sick, cold feeling in her stomach. She took in everything about it, with a sort of hypnotic fascination. The three-cent purple stamp, with wavy cancellation-lines running through it. Then the circular postmark itself, off to the side. It had been posted late, after twelve last night. Where? she wondered. By whom? She could see in her mind's eye an indistinct, furtive figure slinking up to a street mailbox in the dark, a hand hastily thrusting something into the chute, the clang as the slot fell closed again.

She wanted to get it out of here, take it upstairs with her, close the door. But if she carried it away with her unopened, wouldn't that look secretive, wouldn't that call undue attention to it? It was safe enough to open it here in the very room; they never pried in this house, they never asked questions. She knew she could even have left it lying around open after having read it herself, and it would have been safe; nobody would have put a hand to it.

She ran her knife through the flap, slit it.

Mother Hazzard had taken over Hughie's feeding, she had eyes for no one but him. Every mouthful brought forth a paean of praise.

She'd opened the once-folded inner sheet now. The flowers were in the way; they screened the shaking of her hand. So blank it was, so much waste space, so little writing. Just a line across the middle of the paper, where the crease ran.

What are you doing there?

She could feel her chest constricting. She tried to quell the sudden inordinate quickness of her breathing, lest it betray itself.

Mother Hazzard was showing Hughie his plate. "All gone. Hughie ate it all up! Where *is* it?"

She'd lowered it into her lap now. She managed to get it back into its envelope, and fold that over, singly and then doubly, until it fitted into the span of her hand.

"One more and something will snap." And here it was, the one more.

She could feel her self-control ebbing away and didn't know what catastrophic form its loss might take. "I've got to get out of this room," she warned herself. "I've got to get away from this table—now—quickly!"

She stood up suddenly, stumbling a little over her chair. She turned and left the table without a word.

"Patrice, aren't you going to have your coffee?"

"I'll be right down," she said smotheredly from the other side of the doorway. "I forgot something."

She got up there, into her room, and got the door closed.

It was like the bursting of a dam. She hadn't known what form it would take. Tears, she'd thought, or high-pitched hysterical laughter. It was neither. It was anger, a paroxysm of rage, blinded and baffled and helpless.

She went over to the wall and flailed with upraised fists against it, held high over her head. And then around to the next wall and the next and the next, like somebody seeking an outlet, crying out distractedly, "Who are you yourself? Where are you sending them from? Why don't you come out? Why don't you come out in the open? Why don't you come out where I can see you? Why don't you come out and give me a chance to fight back?"

Until at last she'd stopped, wilted and breathing fast with spent emotion. In its wake came sudden determination. There was only one way to fight back, only one way she had to rob the attacks of their power to harm—

She flung the door open. She started down the stairs again. Still as tearless as she'd gone up. She was going fast, she was rippling down them in a quickstep. She was still holding it in her hand. She opened it up, back to its full size, and started smoothing it out as she went.

She came back into the dining room still at the same gait she'd used on the stairs.

"—drank all his milk like a good boy," Mother Hazzard was crooning.

Patrice moved swiftly around the table toward her, stopped short beside her.

"I want to show you something," she said tersely. "I want you to see this."

She put it down on the table squarely in front of her and stood there waiting.

"Just a moment, dear; let me find my glasses," Mother Hazzard purred acquiescently. She probed here and there among the breakfast things. "I know I had them with me when Father was here at the table; we were both reading the paper." She looked over toward the buffet on the other side of her.

Patrice stood there waiting. She looked over at Hughie. He was still holding his spoon, entire fist folded possessively around it. He flapped it at her joyously. Home. Peace.

Suddenly she'd reached over to her own place at the table, picked up the department-store circular still lying there, replaced the first letter with that.

"Here they are, under my napkin. Right in front of me the whole time." Mother Hazzard adjusted them, turned back to her. "Now what was it, dear?" She opened the folder and looked at it.

Patrice pointed. "This pattern, right here. The first one. Isn't it—attractive?"

Behind her back, held in one hand, the abducted missive slowly crumpled, deflated, was sucked between her fingers into compressed invisibility.

QUIETLY and deftly she moved about the dimly lighted room, passing back and forth, and forth and back, with armfuls of belongings from the drawers. Hughie lay sleeping in his crib, and the clock said almost one.

The valise stood open on a chair. Even that wasn't hers. It was the one she'd first used on the train ride here, new-looking as ever, the one with "PH" on its rounded corner. She'd have to borrow it. Just as she was borrowing the articles she picked at random to throw into it. Just as she was borrowing the very clothes she stood in. There were only two things in this whole room with her now that were rightfully hers. That little bundle sleeping quietly there in the crib. And that seventeen cents lying spread out on a scrap of paper on the dresser top.

She took things for him, mostly. Things he needed, things to keep him warm. They wouldn't mind, they wouldn't begrudge that. They loved him almost as much as she did, she reasoned ruefully. She quickened her movements, as if the danger of faltering in purpose lay somewhere along this train of thought if she lingered on it too long.

For herself she took very little, only what was of absolute necessity. Underthings, an extra pair or two of stockings—

Things, things. What did things matter, when your whole world was breaking up and crumbling about you? *Your* world? It wasn't *your* world; it was a world you had no right to be in.

She dropped the lid of the valise, latched it impatiently on what it held, indifferent to whether it held enough, or too much, or too little. A little tongue of white stuff was trapped, left protruding through the seam, and she let it be.

She put on the hat and coat she'd left in readiness across the foot of the bed. The hat without consulting a mirror, though there was one right at her shoulder. She picked up her handbag, and probed into it with questing hand. She brought out a key, the key to this house, and put it down on the dresser. Then she brought out a small change purse and shook it out. A cabbagy cluster of interfolded currency fell out soundlessly, and a sprinkling of coins, these last with a tinkling sound and some rolling about. She swept them all closer together, and then left them there on top of the dresser. Then she picked up the seventeen cents and dropped that into the change purse instead, and replaced it in the handbag, and thrust that under her arm.

She went over beside the crib, then, and lowered its side. She crouched down on a level with the small sleeping face. She kissed it lightly on each eyelid. "I'll be back for you in a minute," she whispered. "I have to take the bag down first and stand it at the door. I can't manage you both on those stairs, I'm afraid." She straightened up, lingered a moment, looking down at him. "We're going for a ride, you and I; we don't know where, and we don't care. Straight out, along the way the trains go. We'll find someone along the road who'll let us in next to him—"

The clock said a little after one now.

She went over to the door, softly opened it, and carried the valise outside with her. She eased it closed behind her, and then she started down the stairs valise in hand, with infinite slowness, as though it weighed a lot. Yet it couldn't have been the valise alone that seemed to pull her arm down so; it must have been the leadenness of her heart.

Suddenly she'd stopped, and allowed the valise to come to rest on the step beside her. They were standing there without a sound, down below her by the front door, the two of them. Father Hazzard and Dr. Parker. She hadn't heard them until now, for they hadn't been saying anything. They must have been standing there in a sort of momentary mournful silence, just preceding leavetaking.

They broke it now, as she stood there unseen, above the bend of the stairs.

"Well, good night, Donald," the doctor said at last, and she saw him put his hand to Father Hazzard's shoulder in an attempt at consolation, then let it trail heavily off again. "Get some sleep. She'll be all right." He opened the door; then he added, "But no excitement, no stress of any kind from now on, you understand that, Donald? That'll be your job, to keep all that away from her. Can I count on you?"

"You can count on me," Father Hazzard said forlornly.

The door closed, and he turned away and started up the stairs, to where she stood riveted. She moved down a step or two around the turn to meet him, leaving the valise behind her, doffed hat and coat flung atop it now.

He looked up and he saw her, without much surprise, without much of anything except a sort of stony sadness.

"Oh, it's you, Patrice," he said dully. "Did you hear him? Did you hear what he just said?"

"Who is it—Mother?"

"She had another of those spells soon after we retired. He's been in there with her for over an hour and a half. It was touch and go, for a few minutes, at first—"

"But Father! Why didn't you—?"

He sat down heavily on the stair step. She sat down beside him, slung one arm about his shoulders.

"Why should I bother you, dear? There wouldn't have been anything you could have— You have the baby on your hands all day long, you need your rest. Besides, this isn't anything new. Her heart's always been weak. Way back before the boys were born—"

"I never knew. You never told me— But is it getting worse?"

"Things like that don't improve as you get on in years," he said gently.

She let her head slant to rest against his shoulder, in compunction.

He patted her hand consolingly. "She'll be all right. We'll see that she is, you and I, between us, won't we?"

She shivered a little, involuntarily, at that.

"It's just that we've got to cushion her against all shocks and upsets," he said. "You and the young fellow, you're about the best medicine for her there is. Just having you around—"

And if in the morning she had asked for Patrice, asked for her grandchild, and he'd had to tell her— She fell strangely silent, looking down at the steps under their feet, but no longer seeing them. And if she'd come out of her room five minutes later, just missing the doctor as he left, she might have brought death into this house, in repayment for all the love that had been lavished on her. Killed the only mother she'd ever known.

He misunderstood her abstraction, pressed her chin with the cleft of his hand. "Now don't take it like that; she wouldn't want you to, you know. And Pat, don't let her know you've found out about it. Let her keep on thinking it's her secret and mine. I know she'll be happier that way."

She sighed deeply. It was a sigh of decision, of capitulation to the inevitable. She turned and kissed him briefly on the side of the head and stroked his hair a couple of times. Then she stood up.

"I'm going up," she said quietly. "Go down and put out the hall light after us, a minute."

He retraced his steps momentarily. She picked up the valise, the coat, the hat, and quietly reopened the door of her own room.

"Good night, Patrice."

"Good night, Father; I'll see you in the morning."

She carried them in with her and closed the door, and in the darkness on the other side she stood still a minute. A silent, choking prayer welled up in her.

"Give me strength, for there's no running away, I see that now. The battle must be fought out here where I stand, and I dare not even cry out."

30

THEN they stopped suddenly. There were no more. No more came. The days became a week, the week became a month. The month lengthened toward two. And no more came.

It was as though the battle had been won without striking a blow. No, she knew that wasn't so; it was as though the battle had been broken off, held in abeyance, at the whim of the crafty, shadowy adversary.

She clutched at straws—straws of attempted comprehension—and they all failed her.

Mother Hazzard said, "Edna Harding got back today; she's been visiting their folks in Philadelphia the past several weeks."

But no more came.

Bill remarked, "I ran into Tom Bryant today; he tells me his older sister Marilyn's been laid up with pleurisy; she only got out of bed for the first time today."

"I *thought* I hadn't seen her."

But no more came.

Caulfield: Population 203,000, she thought. That was what the atlas in the library said. And a pair of hands to each living soul of them. One to hold down the flap of a letter box, on some secret shadowy corner; the other to quickly, furtively slip an envelope through the slot.

No more came. Yet the enigma remained. What was it? Who was it? Or rather, what had it been? Who had it been?

Yet deep in her innermost heart she knew somehow the present tense still fitted it; none other would do. Things like that didn't just happen and then stop. They either never began at all, or else they ran on to their shattering, destructive conclusion.

But in spite of that, security crept back a little; frightened off once and not so bold now as before, but crept tentatively back toward her a little.

In the mornings the world was bittersweet to look at, seeming to hold its breath, waiting to see—

31

MOTHER Hazzard knocked on her door just as she'd finished tucking Hughie in. There wasn't anything exceptional about this; it was a nightly event, the filching of a last grandmotherly kiss just before the light went out. Tonight, however, she seemed to want to talk to Patrice herself. And not to know how to go about it.

She lingered on after she'd kissed him, and the side of the crib had been lifted into place. She stood there somewhat uncertainly, her continued presence preventing Patrice from switching out the light.

There was a moment's awkwardness.

"Patrice."

"Yes, Mother?"

Suddenly she'd blurted it out. "Bill wants to take you to the Country Club dance with him tonight. He's waiting down there now."

Patrice was so completely taken back she didn't answer for a moment, just stood there looking at her.

"He told me to come up and ask you if you'd go with him." Then she rushed on, as if trying to talk her into it by sheer profusion of wordage. "They have one about once each month, you know, and he's going himself, he usually does, and—why don't you get dressed and go with him?" she ended up on a coaxing note.

"But I—I—" Patrice stammered.

"Patrice, you've got to begin sooner or later. It isn't good for you not to. You haven't been looking as well as you might lately. We're a little worried about you. If there's something troubling you— You do what Mother says, dear."

It was apparently an order. Or as close to an order as Mother Hazzard could ever have brought herself to come. She had opened Patrice's closet door, meanwhile, and was peering helpfully inside. "How about this?" She took something down, held it up against herself to show her.

"I haven't very much—"

"It'll do nicely." It landed on the bed. "They're not very formal there. I'll have Bill buy you an orchid or gardenia on the way; that'll dress it up enough. You just go and get the *feel* of it tonight. It'll begin coming back to you little by little." She smiled reassuringly at her. "You'll be in good hands." She patted her on the shoulder as she turned to go outside. "Now that's a good girl. I'll tell Bill you're getting ready."

Patrice overheard her call down to him from above-stairs, a

moment later, without any attempt at modulating her voice: "The answer is yes. I talked her into it. And you be very nice to her, young man, or you'll hear from me."

He was standing waiting for her just inside the door when she came downstairs.

"Am I all right?" she asked uncertainly.

He was suddenly overcome with some sort of awkwardness. "Gee, I—I didn't know how you could look in the evening," he said haltingly.

For the first few moments of the drive, there was a sort of shyness between them, almost as though they'd only just met tonight for the first time. It was very impalpable, but it rode with them. He turned on the radio in the car. Dance music rippled back into their faces. "To get you into the mood," he said.

He stopped, and got out, and came back with an orchid. "The biggest one north of Venezuela," he said. "Or wherever they come from."

"Here, pin it on for me." She selected a place. "Right about here."

Abruptly, he balked at that, for some strange reason. All but shied away bodily. "Oh no, that you do yourself," he said, more forcefully than she could see any reason for.

"I might stick myself," he added lamely as an afterthought. A little too long after.

"Why, you great big coward."

The hand that would have held the pin was a trifle unsteady, she noticed, when he first put it back to the wheel. Then it quieted.

They drove the rest of the way. The rest of the way lay mostly through open country. There were stars overhead.

"I've never *seen* so many!" she marveled.

"Maybe you haven't been looking up enough," he said gently.

Toward the end, just before they got there, a peculiar sort of tenderness seemed to overcome him for a minute. He even slowed the car a little, as he turned to her.

"I want you to be happy tonight, Patrice," he said earnestly. "I want you to be *very* happy."

There was a moment's silence between them; then they picked up speed again.

32

AND for the next one, right after that, the tune they played was "Three Little Words." She remembered that afterward. That least of all things about it, the tune they had been playing at the time. She was dancing it with Bill. For that matter she'd been dancing them all with him, steadily, ever since they'd arrived. She wasn't watching, she wasn't looking around her, she wasn't thinking of anything but the two of them.

Smiling dreamily, she danced. Her thoughts were like a little brook running swiftly but smoothly over harmless pebbles, keeping time with the tinkling music.

I like dancing with him. He dances well; you don't have to keep thinking about your feet. He's turned his face toward me and is looking down at me; I can feel it. Well, I'll look up at him, and then he'll smile at me; but I won't smile back at him. Watch. There, I knew that was coming. I will *not* smile back. Oh well, what if I did? It slipped out before I could stop it. Why shouldn't I smile at him, anyway? That's the way I feel about him: smilingly fond.

A hand touched Bill's shoulder from behind. She could see the fingers slanted downward for a second, on her side of it, without seeing the hand or arm or person it belonged to.

A voice said, "May I cut in on this one?"

And suddenly they'd stopped. Bill had stopped, so she had to, too.

His arms left her. A shuffling motion took place, Bill stepped aside, and there was someone else there in his place. It was like a double exposure, where one person dissolves into another.

Their eyes met, hers and the new pair. His had been waiting for hers, and hers had foolishly run into his. They couldn't move again.

The rest was horror, sheer and unadulterated. Horror such as she'd never known she could experience. Horror under the electric lights. Death on the dance floor. Her body stayed upright, but otherwise she had every feeling of death coursing through it.

"Georgesson's the name," he murmured unobtrusively to Bill. His lips hardly seemed to stir at all. His eyes didn't leave hers.

Bill completed the ghastly parody of an introduction. "Mrs. Hazzard, Mr. Georgesson."

"How do you do?" he said to her.

Somehow there was even worse horror in the trite phrase than there had been in the original confrontation. She was screaming in silent inward panic, her lips locked tight, unable even to speak Bill's name and prevent the transfer.

"May I?" Georgesson said, and Bill nodded, and the transfer had been completed; it was too late.

Then for a moment, blessed reprieve. She felt his arms close about her, and her face sank into the sheltering shadow of his shoulder, and she was dancing again. She no longer had to stand upright, unsupported. There, that was better. A minute to think in. A minute to get your breath in.

The music went on, their dancing went on. Bill's face faded away in the background.

"We've met before, haven't we?"

Keep me from fainting, she prayed, keep me from falling.

He was waiting for his answer.

Don't speak; don't answer him.

"*Who'd* he say you were?"

Her feet faltered, missed.

"Don't make me keep on doing this. I can't. Help me—outside someplace—or I'm—"

"Too warm for you?" he said politely.

She didn't answer. The music was dying. She was dying.

He said, "You went out of step, just then. My fault, I'm afraid."

"Don't—" she whimpered. "Don't—"

The music stopped. They stopped.

His arm left her back, but his hand stayed tight about her wrist, holding her there beside him for a moment.

He said, "There's a veranda outside. Over there, out that way. I'll go out there and wait for you, and we can—go ahead talking."

She hardly knew what she was saying. "I can't— You don't understand—" Her neck wouldn't hold firm; her head kept trying to lob over limply.

"I think I do. I think I understand perfectly. I understand you, and you understand me." Then he added with a grisly sort of emphasis that froze her to the marrow, "I bet we two understand one another better than any other two people in this whole ballroom at the moment."

Bill was coming back toward them from the sidelines.

"I'll be out there where I said. Don't keep me waiting too long, or—I'll simply have to come in and look you up again." His face didn't change. His voice didn't change. "Thanks for the dance," he said as Bill arrived.

He didn't let go her wrist; he transferred it to Bill's keeping, as though she were something inanimate, a doll, and bowed, and turned, and left them.

"Seen him around a few times. Came here stag, I guess." Bill shrugged in dismissal. "Come on."

"Not this one. The one after."

"Are you all right? You look pale."

"It's the lights. I'm going in and powder. You go and dance with someone else."

He grinned at her. "I don't want to dance with someone else."

"Then you go and—and come back for me. The one after."

"The one after."

She watched him from just outside the doorway. He went out front toward the bar. She watched him go in there. She watched him sit down on one of the tall stools. Then she turned and went the other way.

She walked slowly over to the doors leading outside onto the veranda, and stood in one of them, looking out into the fountain-pen-ink blueness of the night. There were wicker chairs, in groups of twos and threes, spaced every few yards, encircling small tables.

The red sequin of a cigarette coal had risen perpendicularly above one, all the way down at the end, imperiously summoning her. Then it shot over the balustrade laterally, cast away in impatient expectancy.

She walked slowly down that way, with the strange feeling of making a journey from which there was to be no return, ever. Her feet seemed to want to take root, hold her back of their own volition.

She came to a halt before him. He slung his hip onto the balustrade, and sat there askew, in insolent informality. He repeated what he'd said inside. "*Who*'d he say you were?"

The stars were moving. They were making peculiar eddying swirls like blurred pinwheels all over the sky.

"You abandoned me," she said with leashed fury. "You abandoned me, with five dollars. Now what do you want?"

"Oh, then we have met before. I *thought* we had. Glad you agree with me."

"Stop it. What do you want?"

"What do I want? I don't want anything. I'm a little confused, that's all. I'd like to be straightened out. The man introduced you under a mistaken name in there."

"What do you want? What are you doing down here?"

"Well, for that matter," he said with insolent urbanity, "what are you doing yourself down here?"

She repeated it a third time. "What do you want?"

"Can't a man show interest in his ex-protégée and child? There's no way of making children ex, you know."

"You're either insane or—"

"You know that isn't so. You wish it were," he said brutally.

She turned on her heel. His hand found her wrist again, flicked around it like a whip. Cutting just as deeply.

"Don't go inside yet. We haven't finished."

She stopped, her back to him now. "I think we have."

"The decision is mine."

He let go of her, but she stayed there where she was. She heard him light another cigarette, saw the momentary reflection from behind her own shoulder.

He spoke at last, voice thick with expelled smoke. "You still haven't cleared things up," he purred. "I'm as mixed up as ever. This Hugh Hazzard married—er—let's say you, his wife, in Paris, a year ago last June fifteenth. I went to considerable expense and trouble to have the exact date on the records there verified. But a year ago last June fifteenth you and I were living in our little furnished room in New York. I have the receipted rent bills to show for this. How could you have been in two such far-apart places at once?" He sighed philosophically. "Somebody's got their dates mixed. Either he had. Or I have." And then very slowly, "Or *you* have."

She winced unavoidably at that. Slowly her head came around, her body still remaining turned from him. Like one who listens hypnotized, against her will.

"It was you who's been sending those—?"

He nodded with mock affability, as if on being complimented on something praiseworthy. "I thought it would be kinder to break it to you gently."

She drew in her breath with an icy shudder of repugnance.

"I first happened on your name among the train casualties, when I was up in New York," he said. He paused. "I went down there and 'identified' you, you know," he went on matter-of-factly. "You have that much to thank me for, at any rate."

He puffed thoughtfully on his cigarette.

"Then I heard one thing and another, and put two and two together. I went back for a while first—got the rent receipts together and one thing and another—and then finally I came on the rest of the way down here, out of curiosity. I became quite confused," he said ironically, "when I learned the rest of the story."

He waited. She didn't say anything. He seemed to take pity on her finally. "I know," he said indulgently, "this isn't the time nor place to—talk over old times. This is a party, and you're anxious to get back and enjoy yourself."

She shivered.

"Is there anywhere I can reach you?"

He took out a notebook, clicked a lighter. She mistakenly thought he was waiting to write at her dictate. Her lips remained frozen.

"Seneca 382," he read from the notebook. He put it away again. His hand made a lazy curve between them. In the stricken silence that followed he suggested after a while, casually, "Lean up against that chair so you don't fall; you don't seem very steady on your feet, and I don't want to have to carry you bodily inside in front of all those people."

She put her hands to the top of the chair-back and stood quiet, head inclined.

The rose-amber haze in the open doorway down at the center of the terrace blotted out for a moment, and Bill was standing there looking for her.

"Patrice, this is our dance."

Georgesson rose for a second from the balustrade in sketchy etiquette, immediately sank back against it.

She made her way toward him, the blue pall of the terrace

covering her uncertainty of step, and went inside with him. His arms took charge of her from that point on, so that she no longer had to be on her own.

"You were both standing there like statues," he said. "He can't be very good company."

She lurched against him in the tendril-like twists of the rumba, her head dropped to rest on his shoulder.

"He isn't very good company," she agreed sickly.

THE phone call came at a fiendishly unpropitious moment.

He'd timed it well. He couldn't have timed it better if he'd been able to look through the walls of the house and watch their movements on the inside. The two men in the family were out. She'd just finished putting Hughie to sleep. She and Mother Hazzard were both up on the second floor, separately. Which meant that she was the only one fully eligible to answer.

She knew at the first instant of hearing it who it was, what it was. She knew too that she'd been expecting it all day, that she'd known it was coming, it was surely coming.

She stood there rooted, unable to move. Maybe it would stop if she didn't go near it, maybe he would tire. But then it would ring again some other time.

Mother Hazzard opened the door of her room and looked out.

Patrice had swiftly opened her own door, was at the head of the stairs, before she'd fully emerged.

"I'll get it on this phone, dear, if you're busy."

"No, never mind, Mother. I was just going downstairs, anyway, so I'll answer it there."

She knew his voice right away. She hadn't heard it for over two years, until just last night, and yet it was again as familiar to her as if she'd been hearing it steadily for months past. Fear quickens the memory.

He was as pleasantly aloof at first as any casual caller on the telephone. "Is this the younger Mrs. Hazzard? Is this Patrice Hazzard?"

"This is she."

"I suppose you know this is Georgesson."

She did know, but she didn't answer that.

"Are you—where you can be heard?"

"I'm not in the habit of answering questions like that. I'll hang up the receiver."

Nothing could seem to make him lose his equanimity. "Don't do that, Patrice," he said urbanely. "I'll ring back again. That'll make it worse. They'll begin wondering who it is keeps on calling so repeatedly. Or, eventually, someone else will answer—you can't stay there by the phone all evening—and I'll give my name if I have to and ask for you." He waited a minute for this to sink in. "Don't you see, it's better for you this way."

She sighed a little, in suppressed fury.

"We can't talk very much over the phone. I think it's better not to, anyway. I'm talking from McClellan's Drugstore, a few blocks from you. My car's just around the corner from there, where it can't be seen. On the left side of Pomeroy Street, just down from the crossing. Can you walk down that far for five or ten minutes? I won't keep you long."

She tried to match the brittle formality of his voice with her own. "I most certainly cannot."

"Of course you can. You need cod-liver-oil capsules for your baby, from McClellan's. Or you feel like a soda, for yourself. I've seen you stop in there more than once, in the evening."

He waited.

"Shall I call back? Would you rather think it over awhile?"

He waited again.

"Don't do that," she said reluctantly, at last.

She could tell he understood: her meaning had been a positive and not a negative one.

She hung up.

She went upstairs again.

Mother Hazzard didn't ask her. They weren't inquisitive that way, in this house. But the door of her room was open. Patrice couldn't bring herself to reenter her own without at least a passing reference. Guilty conscience, this soon? she wondered bitingly.

"That was a Steve Georgesson, Mother," she called in. "Bill and I ran into him there last night. He wanted to know how we'd enjoyed ourselves."

"Well, that was real thoughtful of him, wasn't it?" Then she added, "He must be a decent sort, to do that."

Decent, Patrice thought dismally, easing the door closed after her.

She came out of her room again in about ten minutes' time. Mother Hazzard's door was closed now. She could have gone on down the stairs unquestioned. Again she couldn't do it.

She went over and knocked lightly, to attract attention.

"Mother, I'm going to take a walk down to the drugstore and back. Hughie's out of his talc. And I'd like a breath of air. I'll be back in five minutes."

"Go ahead, dear. I'll say good night to you now, in case I'm asleep by the time you're in again."

She rested her outstretched hand helplessly against the door for a minute. She felt like saying, Mother, don't let me go. Forbid me. Keep me here.

She turned away and went down the stairs. It was her own battle, and no proxies were allowed.

She stopped beside the car, on darkened Pomeroy Street.

"Sit in here, Patrice," he said amiably. He unlatched the door for her, from where he sat, and even palmed the leather cushion patronizingly.

She settled herself on the far side of the seat. Her eyes snapped refusal of the cigarette he was trying to offer her.

"We can be seen."

"Turn this way, toward me. No one'll notice you. Keep your back to the street."

"This can't go on. Now once and for all, for the first time and the last, what is it you want of me, what is this about?"

"Look, Patrice, there doesn't have to be anything unpleasant about this. You seem to be building it up to yourself that way, in your own mind. I have no such— It's all in the way you look at it. I don't see that there has to be any change in the way things were going along—before last night. You were the only one knew before. Now you and I are the only ones know. It ends there. That is, if you want it to."

"You didn't bring me out here to tell me that."

He went off at a tangent. Or what seemed to be a tangent. "I've never amounted to—as much as I'd hoped, I suppose. I mean, I've never gotten as far as I should. As I once expected to. There are lots of us like that. Every once in a while I find myself in difficulties, every now and then I get into a tight squeeze. Little card games with the boys. This and that. You know how it is." He laughed deprecatingly. "It's been going on for years. It's nothing new. But I was wondering if you'd care to do me a favor—this time."

"You're asking me for money."

She almost felt nauseated. She turned her face away.

"I didn't think there were people like you outside of—outside of penitentiaries."

He laughed in good-natured tolerance. "You're in unusual circumstances. That attracts 'people like me.' If you weren't, you *still* wouldn't think there were any; you wouldn't know any different."

"Suppose I go to them now and tell them of this conversation we've just been having, of my own accord. My brother-in-law would go looking for you and beat you within an inch of your life."

"We'll let the relationship stand unchallenged. I wonder why women put such undue faith in a beating-up? Maybe because they're not used to violence themselves. A beating doesn't mean much to a man. Half an hour after it's over, he's as good as he was before."

"You should know," she murmured.

He tapped a finger to the points of three others. "There are three alternatives. You go to them and tell them. Or I go to them and tell them. Or we remain in status quo. By which I mean, you do me a favor, and then we drop the whole thing, nothing further is said. But there isn't any fourth alternative."

He shook his head slightly, in patient disapproval. "You over-dramatize everything so, Patrice. That's the unfailing hallmark of cheapness. You're a cheap girl. That's the basic difference between us. I may be, according to your lights, a rotter, but I have a certain tone. As you visualize it, I'd stride in there, throw my arms out wide in declamation, and blare, 'This girl is not your daughter-in-law!' Not at all. That wouldn't work with people like that. It would overreach itself. All I'd have to do would be to let you accuse yourself out of your own mouth. In their presence. You couldn't refuse the house to me. 'When you were in Paris with Hugh, Patrice, which bank did you live on, Left or Right?' 'What was the name of the boat you made the trip back on, again?' 'Well, when I ran into you over there that day with him—oh, you forgot to mention that we'd already met before, Pat?—why is it you looked so different from what you do today? You don't look like the same girl at all.' Until you crumpled and caved in."

He was capable of it. He was too cold about the whole thing, that was the dangerous feature. No heat, no impulse, no emotion to cloud the issue. Everything planned, plotted, graphed, ahead of time. Drafted. Charted. Every step. Even the notes. She knew their purpose now. Not poison-pen letters at all. They had been important to the long-term scheme of the thing. Psychological warfare, nerve warfare, breaking her down ahead of time, top-pling her resistance before the main attack had even been made. The research trip to New York in-between, to make sure of his own ground, to make sure there was no flaw, to leave her no loophole.

He skipped the edge of his hand off the wheel rim, as if brush-ing off a particle of dust. "There's no villain in this. Let's get rid of the Victorian trappings. It's just a business transaction. It's no different from taking out insurance, really." He turned to her with an assumption of candor that was almost charming for a moment. "Don't you want to be practical about it?"

"I suppose so. I suppose I should meet you on your own ground." She didn't try to project her contempt; it would have failed to reach him, she knew.

"If you get rid of these stuffy fetishes of virtue and villainy, of black and white, the whole thing becomes so simple it's not even worth the quarter of an hour we're giving it here in the car."

"I have no money of my own, Georgesson." Capitulation. Submission.

"They're one of the wealthiest families in town, that's common knowledge. Why be technical about it? Get them to open an account for you. You're not a child."

"I couldn't *ask* them outright to do such a—"

"You don't *ask*. There are ways. You're a woman, aren't you? It's easy enough; a woman knows how to go about those things—"

"I'd like to go now," she said, reaching blindly for the door handle.

"Do we understand one another?" He opened it for her. "I'll give you another ring after a while."

He paused a moment. The threat was so impalpable there was not even a change of inflection in the lazy drawl.

"Don't neglect it, Patrice."

She got out. The crack of the door was the unfelt slap-in-the-face of loathing she gave him.

"Good night, Patrice," he drawled after her amiably.

34

"—Perfectly plain," she was saying animatedly. "It had a belt of the same material, and then a row of buttons down to about here."

She was purposely addressing herself to Mother Hazzard, to the exclusion of the two men members of the family. Well, the topic in itself was excuse enough for that.

"Heaven sakes, why didn't you take it?" Mother Hazzard wanted to know.

"I couldn't do that," she said reluctantly. She stopped a moment; then she added, "Not right—then and there." And played a lot with her fork. And felt low.

They must have thought the expression on her face was wistful disappointment. It wasn't. It was self-disgust.

You don't have to ask openly. There are ways; it's easy enough. A woman knows how to go about those things.

This was one of them now.

How defenseless those who love you are against you, she thought bitterly. How vicious and how criminal it is to trade on that self-imposed defenselessness. As I am doing now. Tricks and traps and wiles, those are for strangers. Those should be used against such only. Not against those who love you; with their guard down, with their eyes trustfully closed. It made her skin crawl in revulsion. She felt indecent, unclean, obscene.

Father Hazzard cut into the conversation. "Why didn't you just charge it up and have it sent? You could have used Mother's account. She deals there a lot."

She let her eyes drop. "I wouldn't have wanted to do that," she said reticently.

"Nonsense—" He stopped suddenly. Almost as though someone had trodden briefly on his foot under the table.

She caught Bill glancing at her. He seemed to be holding the glance a moment longer than was necessary. But before she could verify this, it had stopped, and he resumed bringing the suspended forkful of pie-fill up to his mouth.

"I think I hear Hughie crying," she said, and flung her napkin down and ran out to the stairs to listen.

But in the act of listening upward, she couldn't avoid overhearing Mother Hazzard's guarded voice in the dining room behind her, spacing each word with strictural severity.

"Donald Hazzard, you ought to be ashamed of yourself. Do you menfolk have to be told *every*thing? Haven't you got a grain of tact in your heads?"

35

IN THE morning Father Hazzard had lingered on at the table, she noticed when she came down, instead of leaving early with Bill. He sat quietly reading his newspaper while she finished her coffee. And there was just a touch of secretive self-satisfaction in his attitude, she thought.

He rose in company with her when she got up. "Get your hat and coat, Pat. I want you to come with me in the car. This young lady and I have business downtown," he announced to Mother Hazzard. The latter tried, not altogether successfully, to look blankly bewildered.

"But what about Hughie's feeding?"

"I'll give him his feeding," Mother Hazzard said serenely.

"You'll be back in time for that. I'm just borrowing you."

She got in next to him a moment later, and they started off.

"Did poor Bill have to walk to the office this morning?" she asked.

"Poor Bill indeed!" he scoffed. "Do him good, the big lug. If I had those long legs of his, I'd walk it myself, every morning."

"Where are you taking me?"

"Now just never you mind. No questions. Just wait'll we get there, and you'll see."

They stopped in front of the bank. He motioned her out and led her inside with him. He said something to one of the guards in an aside, and he and she sat down to wait for a moment on a bench.

For the briefest moment only. Then the guard had come back with a noticeable deference. He led them toward a door marked "Manager, Private." Before they could reach it, it had already opened and a pleasant-faced, slightly stout man wearing horn-rimmed spectacles was waiting to greet them.

"Come in and meet my old friend Harve Wheelock," Father Hazzard said to her.

They seated themselves in comfortable leather chairs in the private office, and the two men shared cigars.

"Harve, I've got a new customer for you. This is my boy Hugh's wife. Not that I think your mangy old bank is any good, but—well, you know how it is. Just habit, I reckon."

The manager shook appreciatively all over, as if this were some joke between them that had been going on for years. He winked for Patrice's benefit. "I agree with you there. Sell it to you real cheap."

"How cheap?"

"Quarter of a million." Meanwhile he was penning required entries on a filing form, as though he had all the information called for at his fingers' tips, didn't need to ask anything about it.

Father Hazzard shook his head. "Too cheap. Can't be any good." He offhandedly palmed an oblong of light blue paper onto the desk, left it there facedown.

"You think it over and let me know," the manager said dryly. And to her, reversing his pen, "Sign here, honey."

Forger, she thought scathingly. She handed it back, her eyes downcast. The strip of light blue was clipped to it, and it was sent out. A midget black book came back in its stead.

"Here you are, honey." The manager tendered it to her across his desk.

She opened it and looked at it, unnoticed, while the two resumed their friendly bickering hammer and tongs. It was so spotless, so unused yet. At the top it said, "Mrs. Hugh Hazzard." And there was just one entry, under today's date. A deposit: "5000.00."

36

SHE stood there holding the small round canister, staring frozenly at it as though she couldn't make out what was in it. She'd been holding it like that for long moments, without actually seeing it. She tilted it at last and dumped its contents into the washbowl. It had been better than half full.

She went out, and closed the door, and went across the hall, and knocked softly.

"I'm stepping out for just a moment, Mother. Hughie upset his whole can of talc in the bath just now, and I want to get another before I forget."

"All right, dear. The walk'll do you good. Oh—bring me back

a bottle of that shampoo while you're in there, dear. I'm on the last of it now."

She got that slightly sickened feeling she was beginning to know so well. It was so easy to fool those who loved you. But who were you really fooling—them or yourself?

His arm was draped negligently atop the car door, elbow out. The door fell open. He made way for her by shifting leisurely over on the seat, without offering to rise. His indolent taking of her for granted was more scathingly insulting than any overt rudeness would have been.

"I'm sorry I had to call. I thought you'd forgotten about our talk. It's been more than a week now."

"Forgotten?" she said dryly. "I wish it were that easy."

"I see you've become a depositor of the Standard Trust since our last meeting."

She shot him an involuntary look of shock, without answering.

"Five thousand dollars."

She drew a quick breath.

"Tellers will chat for a quarter cigar." He smiled. "Well?"

"I haven't any money with me. I haven't used the account yet. I'll have to cash a check in the morning and—"

"They give a checkbook with each account, don't they? And you have that with you, most likely—"

She gave him a look of unfeigned surprise.

"I have a fountain pen right here in my pocket. I'll turn on the dashboard lights a minute. Let's get it over and done with; the quickest way's the best. Now, I'll tell you what to write. 'To Stephen Georgesson. Not to Cash or Bearer. Five hundred.' "

"Five hundred?"

"That's academic."

She didn't understand what he meant and was incautious enough to let him go on past that point without stopping him.

"That's all. And then your signature. The date, if you want."

She stopped short. "I can't do this."

"I'm sorry, you'll have to. I don't want it any other way. I won't accept cash."

"But this passes through the bank with both our names on it, mine as payer, yours as payee."

"There's such a flood of checks passing through the bank every month, it's not even likely to be noticed. It could be a debt of Hugh's, you know, that you're settling up for him."

"Why are you so anxious to have a check?" she asked irresolutely.

A crooked smile looped one corner of his mouth. "Why should you object, if I don't? It's to your advantage, isn't it? I'm playing right into your hands. It comes back into your possession after it clears the bank. After that you're holding tangible evidence of this—of blackmail—against me if you should ever care to prosecute. Which is something you haven't got so far. Remember, up to this point, it's just your word against mine. I can deny this whole thing happened. Once this check goes through, you've got living proof."

He said, a little more tartly than he'd yet spoken to her, "Shall we get through? You're anxious to get back. And I'm anxious to pull out of here."

She handed him the completed check and pen.

He was smiling again now. He waited until she'd stepped out and he'd turned on the ignition. He said above the low throb of the motor, "Your thinking isn't very clear, nor very quick, is it? This check is evidence against *me*, that *you're* holding, if it clears the bank and returns to you. But if it doesn't—if it's kept out, and never comes up for payment at all—then it's evidence against *you*, that *I'm* holding."

The car glided off and left her standing behind looking after it in her shattered consternation.

37

SHE all but ran toward the car along the night-shaded street, as if fearful it might suddenly glide into motion and escape her, instead of directing her steps toward it grudgingly as she had the two previous times. She clung to the top of the door with both hands when she'd reached it, as if in quest of support.

"I can't stand this! What are you trying to do to me?"

He was smugly facetious. His brows went up. "Do? I haven't done anything to you. I haven't been near you. I haven't seen you in the last three weeks."

"The check wasn't debited."

"Oh, you've had your bank statement. That's right, yesterday was the first of the month. I imagine you've had a bad twenty-four hours. I must have overlooked it—"

"No," she said with fierce rancor, "you're not the kind would overlook anything like that, you vicious leech! Haven't you done enough to me? What are you trying to do, drive me completely out of my mind—"

His manner changed abruptly, tightened. "Get in," he said crisply. "I want to talk to you. I'll drive you around for a quarter of an hour or so."

"I can't *ride* with you. How can you ask me to do that?"

"We can't just stand still in this one place, talking it over. That's far worse. We've done that twice already. We can circle the lake drive once or twice; there's no one on it at this hour and no stops. Turn your collar up across your mouth."

"Why are you holding the check? What are you meaning to do?"

"Wait until we get there," he said.

Then when they had, he answered her, coldly, dispassionately, as though there had been no interruption. "I'm not interested in five hundred dollars."

She was beginning to lose her head. Her inability to fathom his motives was kindling her to panic. "Give it back to me, then, and I'll give you more. I'll give you a thousand. Only, give it back to me."

"I don't want to be *given* more. I don't want to be *given* any amount. Don't you understand? I want the money to belong to *me*, in my own right."

Her face was suddenly stricken white. "I don't understand. What are you trying to say to me?"

"I think you're beginning to, by the look on your face." He fumbled in his pocket, took something out. An envelope, already sealed and stamped for mailing. "You asked me where the check was. It's in here. Here, read what it says on it. No, don't take it out of my hand. Just read it from where you are."

Mr. Donald Hazzard
Hazzard and Loring
Empire Building
Caulfield

"No—" She couldn't articulate, could only shake her head convulsively.

"I'm mailing it to him at his office, where you can't intercept it." He returned it to his pocket. "The last mail collection, here in Caulfield, is at nine each night. You may not know that, but I've been making a study of those things recently. There's a mailbox on Pomeroy Street, just a few feet from where I've been parking the last few times I've met you. It's dark and inconspicuous around there, and I'll use that one. It takes the carrier until nine-fifteen to reach it, however; I've timed him several nights in a row and taken the average."

He silenced her with his hand, went on: "Now, if you reach there before the carrier does, this envelope stays out of the chute. If you're not there yet when he arrives, I drop it in. You have a day's grace, until nine-fifteen tomorrow night."

"But what do you want me to be there for? You said you didn't want more—"

"We're going to take a ride out to Hastings, that's the next town over. I'm taking you to a justice of the peace there, and he's going to make us man and wife."

He slowed the car as her head lurched soddenly back over the top of the seat for a moment.

"I didn't think they swooned anymore—" he began. Then as he

saw her straighten again with an effort and pass the back of her hand blurredly before her eyes, he added, "Oh, I see they don't; they just get a little dizzy, is that it?"

"Why are you doing this to me?" she said smotheredly.

"There are several good reasons I can think of. It's a good deal safer, from my point of view, than the basis we've been going on so far. There's no chance of anything backfiring. A wife, the law-books say, cannot testify against her husband. That means that any lawyer worth his fee can whisk you off the stand before you can so much as open your mouth. And then there are more practical considerations. The old couple aren't going to be around forever, you know. The old lady's life is hanging by a thread. And the old man won't last any time without her. Old Faithful, I know the type. When they go, you and Bill share unequally between you— Don't look so horrified; that lawyer of theirs hasn't exactly talked, but this is a small town, those things sort of seep around without even benefit of word of mouth. I can wait that year, or even two or three if I have to. The law gives a husband one-third of his wife's property. Three-quarters of—I may be underestimating, but roughly I'd say four hundred thousand, that's three hundred thousand. And then a third of that again— Don't cover your ears like that, Patrice; you look like someone out of a Marie Corelli novel."

He braked. "You can get out here, Patrice. This is close enough." And then he chuckled a little, watching her flounder to the pavement. "Are you sure you're able to walk steady? I wouldn't want to have them think I'd plied you with—"

The last thing he said was, "Make sure your clock isn't slow, Patrice. Because the United States Mail is always on time."

38

THE headlight beams of his car kept slashing up the road ahead of them like plowshares, seeming to cast aside its topsoil of darkness, reveal its borax-like white fill, and spill that out all over the roadway. Then behind them the livid furrows would heal again into immediate darkness.

It seemed hours they'd been driving like this, in silence yet acutely aware of one another. Trees went by, dimly lit up from below, along their trunks, by the passing reflection of their headlight wash, into a sort of ghostly incandescence. Then at times there weren't any trees, they fell back, and a plushy black evenness took their place—fields or meadows, she supposed—that smelled sweeter. Clover. It was beautiful country around here;

too beautiful for anyone to be in such a hell of suffering in the midst of it.

Roads branched off at times, too, but they never took them. They kept to this wide, straight one they were on.

They passed an indirectly lighted white sign, placed at right angles to the road so that it could be read as you came up to it. It said "Welcome to Hastings," and then underneath, "Population—" and some figures too small to catch before they had already gone by.

She glanced briefly after it, in a sort of fascinated horror.

He'd apparently seen her do it, without looking directly at her. "That's across the state line," he remarked dryly. "Travel broadens one, they say." It was nine-forty-five now according to her wristwatch. It had taken them only half an hour's drive to get here.

They passed through the town's nuclear main square. A drugstore was still open, two of the old-fashioned jars of colored water that all drugstore windows featured once upon a time flashing emerald and mauve at them as they went by. A motion-picture theater was still alive inside, but dying fast externally, its marquee already dark, its lobby dim.

He turned up one of the side streets, a tunnel under leafy shade trees, its houses all set back a lawn-spaced distance so that they were almost invisible in the night shade from the roadway. A dim light peering through from under the recesses of an ivy-covered porch seemed to attract him. He shunted over to the walk suddenly, and back a little, and stopped opposite it.

They sat for a while.

Then he got out on his side, came around to hers, and opened the door beside her.

"Come in," he said briefly.

She didn't move, she didn't answer.

"Come on in with me. They're waiting."

She didn't answer, didn't move.

"Don't just sit there like that. We had this all out before, back at Caulfield. Move. Say something, will you?"

"What do you want me to say?"

He gave the door an impatient slap-to again, as if in momentary reprieve. "Get yourself together. I'll go over and let them know we got here."

She watched him go, in a sort of stupor, as though this were happening to someone else; heard his tread go up the wooden plank walk that led up to the house. She could even hear the ring of the bell, from within the house, all the way out here where she was. It was no wonder, it was so quiet. Just little winged things buzzing and humming in a tree overhead.

She wondered, How does he know I won't suddenly start the car and drive off? She answered that herself: He knows I won't. He knows it's too late for that. As I know it. The time for stopping, for drawing back, for dashing off, that was long ago. So long ago. Long before tonight. That was in the compartment on the train coming here, when the wheels tried to warn me. That was when the first note came. That was when the first phone call came, the first walk down to the drugstore. I am as safely held fast here as though I were manacled to him.

She could hear their voices now. A woman saying, "No, not at all; you made very good time. Come right in."

The doorway remained open, lighted. Whoever had been standing in it had withdrawn into the house. He was coming back toward her now. The sound of his tread along the wooden walk.

She gripped the edge of the car seat with her hands, dug them in under the leather cushions.

He was up to her now, standing there.

"Come on, Patrice," he said casually.

That was the full horror of it, his casualness, his matter-of-factness. He wasn't acting the part.

She spoke quietly too, as quietly as he, but her voice was as thin and blurred as a thrumming wire.

"I can't do it. Georgesson, don't ask me to do this."

"Patrice, we've been all over this. I told you the other night, and it was all settled then."

She covered her face with cupped hands, quickly uncovered it again. She kept using the same four words; they were the only ones she could think of. "But I can't do it. Don't you understand? I can't *do* it."

"There's no impediment. You're not married to anyone. Even in your assumed character, you're not married to anyone, much less as yourself. I investigated all that in New York."

"Steve. Listen, I'm calling you Steve."

"That doesn't melt me," he assured her jocosely. "That's my name; I'm supposed to be called that." He lidded his eyes at her. "It's my *given* name, not one that I took for myself—*Patrice*."

"Steve, I've never pleaded with you before. In all these months, I've taken it like a woman. Steve, if there's anything human in you at all I can appeal to—"

"I'm only too human. That's why I like money as much as I do. But your wires are crossed. It's my very humanness, for that reason, that makes your appeal useless. Come on, Patrice. You're wasting time."

She cowered away edgewise along the seat. He drummed his fingers on the top of the door and laughed a little.

"Why this horror of marriage? Let me get to the bottom of your aversion. Maybe I can reassure you. There is no personal appeal involved; you haven't any for me. I've got only contempt for you, for being the cheap, tricky little fool you are. I'm leaving you on the doorstep of your ever-loving family again, just as soon as we get back to Caulfield. This is going to be a paper marriage, in every sense of the word. But it's going to stick, it's going to stick to the bitter end. Now does that take care of your mid-Victorian qualms?"

She cast the back of her hand across her eyes as though a blow had just blinded her.

He wrenched the door open.

"They're waiting for us in there. Come on, you're only making it worse."

He was beginning to harden against her. Her opposition was commencing to inflame him against her. It showed inversely, in a sort of lethal coldness.

"Look, my friend, I'm not going to drag you in there by the hair. The thing isn't worth it. I'm going inside a minute and call the Hazzard house from here, and tell them the whole story right now. Then I'll drive you back where I got you from. They can have you—if they want you anymore." He leaned toward her slightly across the door. "Take a good look at me. Do I look like I was kidding?"

He meant it. It wasn't an empty bluff, with nothing behind it. It might be a threat that he would prefer not to have to carry out, but it wasn't an idle threat. She could see that in his eyes, in the cold sullenness in them, the dislike of herself she read in them.

He turned and left the car side and went up the plank walk again, more forcefully, more swiftly, than he'd trod it before.

"Excuse me, could I trouble you for a minute—" she heard him start to say as he entered the open doorway; then the rest was blurred as he went deeper within.

She struggled out, clinging to the flexing door like somebody walking in his sleep. Then she wavered up the plank walk and onto the porch, and the ivy rustled for a minute as she teetered soddenly against it. Then she went on toward the oblong of light projected by the open doorway, and inside. It was like struggling through knee-deep water.

A middle-aged woman met her in the hallway.

"Good evening. Are you Mrs. Hazzard? He's in here."

She took her to a room on the left, parted an old-fashioned pair of sliding doors. He was standing in there, with his back to them, beside an old-fashioned telephone box bracketed to the wall.

"Here's the young lady. You can both come into the study when you're ready."

Patrice drew the doors together behind her again. "Steve," she said.

He turned around and looked at her, then turned back again.

"Don't—you'll kill her," she pleaded.

"The old all die sooner or later."

"Has it gone through yet?"

"They're ringing Caulfield for me now."

It wasn't any sleight-of-hand trick. His finger wasn't anywhere near the receiver hook, holding it shut down. He was in the act of carrying it out.

A choking sound broke in her throat.

He looked around again, less fully than before. "Have you decided once and for all?"

She didn't nod; she simply let her eyelids drop closed for a minute.

"Operator," he said, "cancel that call. It was a mistake." He replaced the receiver.

She felt a little sick and dizzy, as when you've just looked down from some great height and then drawn back again.

He went over to the sliding doors and swung them vigorously back. "We're ready," he called into the study across the hall.

He crooked his arm toward her, backhand, contemptuously tilting up his elbow for her to take, without even looking around at her as he did so.

She came forward, and they went toward the study together, her arm linked in his. Into where the man was waiting to marry them.

39

IT WAS on the way back that she knew she was going to kill him. Knew she must, knew it was the only thing left to be done now. She should have done it sooner, she told herself. Long before this—that first night as she sat with him in his car. It would have been that much better. Then this, tonight's ultimate horror and degradation, would at least have been avoided. She hadn't thought of it then; that was the one thing that had never occurred to her. It had always been flight, escape from him in some other way; never safety in this way—his removal.

But she knew she was going to do it, now. Tonight.

Not a word had passed between them, all this way, ever since leaving the justice's house. Why should one? What was there to say? What was there to do now—except this one final thing, that came to her opposite a white-stockinged telegraph pole, about four miles out of Hastings. Just like that it came: click, snap, and it was there. As though she had passed through some electric-eye beam stretched across the road, there from that particular telegraph pole. On the one side of it, still, just passive despair, fatalism. On the other, full-grown decision, remorseless, irrevocable: I'm going to kill him. Tonight. Before this night ends, before the light comes again.

Neither of them said anything. He didn't, because he was content. He'd done what he'd set out to do. He did whistle lightly, once, for a short while, but then he stopped that again. She didn't say anything, because she was undone. Destroyed, in the fullest sense of the word. She'd never felt like this before. She didn't even feel pain of mind anymore. Struggle was ended. She was numb now. She'd even had more feeling left in her after the train crash than now.

She rode all the way with her eyes held shut. Like a woman returning from a funeral, at which everything worth keeping has been interred, and to whom nothing left above ground is worth looking at any longer.

She heard him speak at last. "There, was that so bad?" he said.

She answered him mechanically, without opening her eyes. "Where are you? What do you want me to do now?"

"Exactly nothing. You go on just as you were before. This is something between the two of us. And I want it to stay that way, understand? Not a word to the Family. Not until I'm ready. It'll be Our Little Secret, yours and mine."

He was afraid if he took her with him openly, they'd change the will, she supposed. And afraid if he left her with them, and they learned of it, they'd have it annulled for her.

How did you kill a man? There was nothing here, no way. The country was flat, the road level, straight. If she snatched at the wheel, tried to throw the car out of control, nothing much would happen. You needed steep places, hairbreadth turns. And the car was only trundling along, not going fast. It would only roll off into the dirt maybe, strike a telegraph pole, shake them up a little.

Besides, even if that had been the feasible way, she didn't want to die with him. She only wanted him to die. She had a child she was devoted to, a man she loved. She wanted to live. She'd always had an unquenchable will to live, all her life; she still had it now. Numbed as she was, it was still flickering stubbornly inside her. Nothing could put it out, or—she would already have contemplated another alternative, probably, before now.

Oh God, she cried out in her mind, if I only had a—

And in that instant, she knew how to do it. Knew how she was going to do it. For the next word-symbol flashing before her senses was "gun," and as it appeared, it brought its own answer to the plea.

In the library, at home. There was one in there, somewhere.

A brief scene came back to mind, from many months ago. Buried until now, to suddenly reappear, as clear as if it had just taken place a moment ago. The reading lamp, comfortably lit and casting its cheerful glow. Father Hazzard, sitting there by it, lingering late over a book. The others gone to bed, all but herself. She the last one to leave him. A brief kiss on his forehead.

"Shall I lock up for you?"

"No, you run along. I will, in a moment."

"You won't forget, though?"

"No, I won't forget." And then he'd chuckled, in that dry way of his. "Don't be nervous, I'm well protected down here. There's a revolver in one of the drawers right by me here. We keep it specially for burglars. That was Mother's idea, once, years ago—and there hasn't been hide nor hair of one in all the time since."

She'd laughed at this melodramatic drollery and told him quite truthfully, "It wasn't prowlers I was thinking of, but a sudden rainstorm in the middle of the night and Mother's best drapes."

She'd laughed. But now she didn't.

Now she knew where there was a gun.

You crooked your finger through. You pulled. And you had peace, you had safety.

They stopped, and she heard the car door beside her clack open. She raised her eyes. They were in a leafy tunnel of the street trees. She recognized the symmetrical formation of the trees, the lawn slopes on either side of them, the dim contours of the private homes in the background. They were on her own street, but further over, about a block away from the house. He was being tactful, letting her out at a great enough distance from her own door to be inconspicuous.

He was sitting there, waiting for her to take the hint and get out. She looked at her watch mechanically. Not even eleven yet. It must have been around ten when it happened. It had taken them forty minutes coming back; they'd driven slower than going out.

He'd seen her do it. He smiled satirically. "Doesn't take long to marry, does it?"

It doesn't take long to die, either, she thought smolderingly.

"Don't you—don't you want me to come with you?" she whispered.

"What for?" he said insolently. "I don't want you. I just want what eventually—comes with you. You go upstairs to your unsullied little bed. (I trust it is, anyway. With this Bill in the house.)"

She could feel heat in her face. But nothing much mattered, nothing counted. Except that the gun was a block away, and he was here. And the two of them had to meet.

"Just stay put," he advised her. "No unexpected little trips out of town now, Patrice. Unless you want me to suddenly step forward and claim paternity of the child. I have the law on my side now, you know. I'll go straight to the police."

"Well—will you wait here a minute? I'll—I'll be right out. I'll get you some money. You'll need some—until—until we get together again."

"Your dowry?" he said ironically. "So soon? Well, as a matter of fact, I don't. Some of the men in this town play very poor cards. Anyway, why give me what's already mine? Piecemeal. I can wait. Don't do me any favors."

She stepped down reluctantly.

"Where can I reach you, in case I have to?"

"I'll be around. You'll hear from me, every now and then. Don't be afraid of losing me."

No, it had to be tonight, tonight, she kept telling herself grimly. Before the darkness ended and the daybreak came. If she waited, she'd lose her courage. This surgery had to be performed at once, this cancer on her future removed.

No matter where he goes in this city tonight, she vowed, I'll track him down, I'll find him, and I'll put an end to him. Even if I have to destroy my own self doing it. Even if I have to do it in sight of a hundred people.

The car door swung closed. He tipped his hat satirically.

"Good night, Mrs. Georgesson. Pleasant dreams to you. Try sleeping on a piece of wedding cake. If you haven't wedding cake, try a hunk of stale bread. You'll be just as crummy either way."

The car sidled past her. Her eyes fastened on the rear license plate, clove to it, memorized it, even as it went skimming past. It dwindled. The red taillight coursed around the next corner and disappeared. But it seemed to hang there before her eyes, like a ghost plaque, suspended against the night, for long minutes after.

NY09231

Then that, too, dimmed and went out.

Somebody was walking along the quiet night sidewalk, very close by. She could hear the chip-chipping of the high heels. That was she. The trees were moving by her, slowly rearward. Somebody was climbing terraced flagstone steps. She could hear the gritty sound of the ascending tread. That was she. Somebody was standing before the door of the house now. She could see the darkling reflection in the glass opposite her. It moved as she moved. That was she.

She opened her handbag and felt inside it for her door key. Hers, was good. The key they'd given her. It was still there. For some reason this surprised her. Funny to come home like this, just as though nothing had happened to you, and feel for your key, and put it into the door, and—and go into the house. To *still* come home like this, and *still* go into the house.

I have to go in here, she defended herself. My baby's asleep in this house. He's asleep upstairs in it, right now. This is where I have to go; there isn't any other place for me to go.

She remembered how she'd had to lie, earlier tonight, asking Mother Hazzard to mind Hughie for her while she visited a new friend. Father had been at a business meeting, and Bill had been out.

She put on the lights in the lower hall. She closed the door. Then she stood there a minute, her breath rising and falling, her back supine against the door. It was so quiet, so quiet in this house. People sleeping, people who trusted you. People who didn't expect you to bring home scandal and murder to them, in return for all their goodness to you.

She stood there immobile. So quiet, so still, there was no guessing what she had come back here for, what she had come back here to do.

Nothing left. Nothing. No home, no love, even no child anymore. She'd even forfeited that prospective love, tarnished it for a later day. She'd lose him too; he'd turn against her when he was old enough to know this about her.

He'd done all this to her, one man. It wasn't enough that he'd done it once; he'd done it twice now. He'd wrecked two lives for her. He'd smashed up the poor inoffensive seventeen-year-old simpleton from San Francisco who had had the bad luck to stray his way. Smashed her up, and wiped his feet all over her five-and-ten-cent-store dreams, and spit on them. And now he'd smashed up the cardboard lady they called Patrice.

He wouldn't smash up anybody more!

A tortured grimace disfigured her face for a moment. The back of her wrist went to her forehead, clung there. An inhalation of terrible softness, yet terrible resolve, shook her entire frame. Then she tottered on the bias toward the library entrance, like a comic drunk lacking in sufficient coordination to face squarely in the direction in which he is hastening.

She put on the big reading lamp in there, center table.

She went deliberately to the cellarette, and opened that, and poured some brandy and downed it. It seemed to blast its way down into her, but she quelled it with a resolute effort.

Ah, yes, you needed that when you were going to kill a man.

She went looking for the gun. She tried the table drawers first, and it was not in there. Only papers and things, in the way. But he'd said there was one in here, that night, and there must be, somewhere in this room. They never told you anything that was untrue, even lightly; he, nor Mother, nor—nor Bill either for that matter. That was the big difference between them and her. That was why they had peace—and she had none.

She tried Father Hazzard's desk next. The number of drawers and cubicles was greater, but she sought them all out one by one. Something glinted as she moved a heavy business ledger aside in the bottommost under-drawer, and there it lay, thrust in at the back.

She took it out. Its inoffensive look, at first, was almost a disappointment. So small, to do so great a thing. To take away a life. Burnished nickel, and bone. And that fluted bulge in the middle, she supposed, was where its hidden powers of death lay. In her unfamiliarity, she pounded at its back with the heel of her hand, and strained at it, trying to get it open, risking a premature discharge, hoping only that if she kept fingers clear of the trigger she would avert one. Suddenly, with astonishing ease at the accidental right touch, it had broken downward, it slanted open. Round black chambers, empty.

She rummaged in the drawer some more. She found the same small cardboard box, half-noted in her previous search, that she had hastily cast aside. Inside, cotton wool, as if to hold some very perishable medicinal capsule. But instead, steel-jacketed, snub-nosed, the cartridges. Only five of them.

She pressed them home, one by one, into the pits they were meant for. One chamber remained empty.

She closed the gun.

She wondered if it would fit into her handbag. She tried it spadewise, the flat side up, and it went in.

She closed the handbag, and took it with her, and went out of the room, went out to the back of the hall.

She took out the classified directory, looked under "Garages."

He might leave it out in the streets overnight. But she didn't think he would. He was the kind who prized his cars and his hats and his watches. He was the kind of man prized everything but his women.

The garages were alphabetized, and she began calling them alphabetically.

"Have you a New York car there for the night, license 09231?"

At the third place the night attendant came back and said, "Yes, we have. It was just brought in a few minutes ago."

"Mr. Georgesson?"

"Yeah, that's right. What about it, lady? Whaddya want from us?"

"I—I was out in it just now. The young man just brought me home in it. And I find I left something with him. I have to get hold of him. Please, it's important. Will you tell me where I can reach him?"

"We ain't supposed to do that, lady."

"But I can't get in. He has my door key, don't you understand?"

"Whyn'tcha ring your doorbell?" the gruff voice answered.

"You fool!" she exploded, her fury lending her plausible eloquence. "I wasn't supposed to be out with him in the first place! I don't want to attract any attention. I *can't* ring the doorbell!"

"I getcha, lady," the voice jeered, with that particular degree of greasiness she'd known it would have, "I getcha." And a double tongue-click was given for punctuation. "Wait'll I check up."

He left. He got on again, said, "He's been keeping his car with us for some time now. The address on our records is 110 Decatur Road. I don't know if that's still—"

But she'd hung up.

SHE used her own key to unlock the garage door. The little road-
ster that Bill habitually used was out, but the big car, the sedan,
was in there. She backed it out. Then she got out a moment, went
back to refasten the garage door.

There was the same feeling of unreality about this as before; a
sort of dream fantasy, a state of somnambulism, yet with overall
awareness. The chip-chip of footsteps along the cement garage
driveway that were someone else's, yet were her own—sounding
from under her. It was as though she had experienced a violent
personality split, and one of her selves, aghast and helpless,
watched a phantom murderess issue from the cleavage and start
out upon her deadly quest. She could only pace this dark thing,

this other self, could not recapture nor reabsorb it, once loosed. Hence (perhaps) the detached objectivity of the footsteps, the mirror-like reproduction of her own movements.

Reentering the car, she backed it into the street, reversed it, and let it flow forward. Not violently, but with the suave pickup of a perfectly possessed driver. Some other hand, not hers—so firm, so steady, so pure—remembered to reach for the door latch and draw the door securely closed with a smart little clout.

Outside, the streetlights went spinning by like glowing bowls coming toward her down a bowling alley. But each shot was a miss, they went alternately too far out to this side, too far out to that. With herself and the car, the kingpin in the middle that they never knocked down.

She thought, That must be Fate, bowling against me. But I don't care, let them come.

Then the car had stopped again. So easy it was to go forth to kill a man.

She didn't study it closely to see what it was like. It didn't matter what it was like. She was going in there; it was going to happen there.

She pedaled the accelerator again, went on past the door and around the corner. There she made a turn, for the right-of-way was against her, pointed the car forward to the way from which she had just come, brought it over against the sidewalk, stopped it there, just out of sight.

She took up her bag from beside her on the seat, as a woman does who is about to leave a car, secured it under her arm.

She shut off the ignition and got out. She walked back around the corner, to where she'd just come from, with the quick, preoccupied gait of a woman returning home late at night, who hastens to get off the street. One has seen them that way many times; minding their own business with an added intentness, for they know they run a greater risk of being accosted then than during the daylight hours.

She found herself alone on a gloomy nocturnal strip of sidewalk in front of a long rambling two-story structure, hybrid, half commercial and half living quarters. The ground floor was a succession of unlighted storefronts, the upper a long row of windows. The white shape of a milk bottle stood on the sill of one of these. One was lighted, but with the shade drawn. Not the one with the milk bottle.

Between two of the storefronts, recessed, almost secretive in its inconspicuousness, there was a single-panel door, with a waffle-pattern of multiple small panes set into it. They could be detected because there was a dim hall light somewhere beyond them, doing its best to overcome the darkness.

She went over to it and tried it, and it swung out without any demur; it had no lock, was simply a closure for appearances' sake. Inside there was a rusted radiator, and a cement stair going up, and at the side of this, just as it began, a row of letter boxes and push buttons. His name was on the third she scanned, but not in its own right, superimposed on the card of the previous tenant, left behind. He had pencil-scratched the name off and then put in his own underneath: "S. Georgesson." He didn't print very well.

He didn't do anything very well, except smash up people's lives. He did that very well, he was an expert.

She went on up the stairs and followed the hall. It was a jerry-built, makeshift sort of a place. During the war shortage they must have taken the attic or storage-space part of the stores below and rigged it up into these flats.

What a place to live, she thought dimly.

What a place to die, she thought remorselessly.

She could see the thin line the light made under his door. She knocked, and then she knocked again, softly like the first time. He had his radio on in there. She could hear that quite distinctly through the door.

She raised her hand and smoothed back her hair, while waiting. You smoothed your hair—if it needed it—just before you were going to see anyone, or anyone was going to see you. That was why she did it now.

They said you were frightened at a time like this. They said you were keyed-up to an ungovernable pitch. They said you were blinded by fuming emotion.

They said. What did they know? She felt nothing. Neither fear nor excitement nor blind anger. Only a dull, aching determination all over.

He didn't hear, or he wasn't coming to open. She tried the knob, and this door too, like the one below, was unlocked; it gave inward. Why shouldn't it be? she reasoned. What did he have to fear from others? They didn't take from him; he took from them.

She closed it behind her, to keep this just between the two of them.

He didn't meet her eyes. The room was reeking with his presence, but it was a double arrangement, bed and living quarters, and he must be in the one just beyond, must have just stepped in as she arrived outside. She could see offside light coming through the opening.

The coat and hat he'd worn in the car with her tonight were slung over a chair, the coat broadside across its seat, the hat atop that. A cigarette that he'd incompletely extinguished a few short moments ago was in a glass tray, stubbornly smoldering away. The drink that he'd started, then left, and was coming back to finish any second now—the drink with which he was celebrating tonight's successful enterprise—stood there on the edge of the table. The white block of its still-unmelted ice cube peered through the side of the glass, through the straw-colored whiskey it floated in.

The sight of it brought back a furnished room in New York. He took his drinks weak; he liked them strong, but he took them weak when it was his own whiskey he was using. "There's always another one coming up," he used to say to her.

There wasn't now. This was his last drink. (You should have made it stronger, she thought to herself wryly.)

Some sort of gritty noise was bothering her. A pulsation, a discord of some sort. It was meant for music, but no music could have reached her as music, as she was now. The hypertension of her senses filtered it into a sound somewhat like a scrubbing brush being passed over a sheet of ribbed tin. Or maybe, it occurred to her, it was on the inside of her and not outside anywhere.

No, there it was. He had a small battery-portable standing against the side wall. She went over to it.

"*Che gelida mannina—*" some far-off voice was singing; she didn't know what that meant. She only knew that this was no love scene; this was a death scene.

Her hand gave a brutal little wrench, like wringing the neck of a chicken, and there was a stupor of silence in his two shoddy rooms. This one out here, and that one in there.

Now he'd step out to see who had done that.

She turned to face the opening. She raised her handbag frontally to her chest. She undid it, and took out the gun, and fitted her hand around it, the way her hand was supposed to go. Without flurry, without a tremor, every move in perfect coordination.

She sighted the gun toward the opening.

"Steve," she said to him, at no more than room-to-room conversational pitch in the utter stillness. "Come out here a second. I want to see you."

No fear, no love, no hate, no anything at all.

He didn't come. Had he seen her in a mirror? Had he guessed? Was he that much of a coward, cringing away even from a woman?

The fractured cigarette continued to unravel into smoke skeins. The ice cube continued to peer through the highball glass, foursquare and uneroded.

She went toward the opening.

"Steve," she rasped. "Your wife is here. Here to see you."

He didn't stir, he didn't answer.

She made the turn of the doorway, gun wheeling before her like some sort of foreshortened steering gear. The second room was not parallel to the first; it was over at a right angle to it. It was very small, just an alcove for sleeping in. It had a bulb up above, as though a luminous blister had formed on the calcimined surface of the ceiling. There was also a lamp beside the iron cot, and that was lit as well, but it was upside down. It was standing on its head on the floor, its extension wire grotesquely looped in air.

She'd caught him in the act of getting ready for bed. His shirt was lying over the foot of the cot. That was all he'd taken off. And now he was trying to hide from her, down on the floor somewhere, below cot level, on the far side of it. His hand peered over it—he'd forgotten that it showed—clutching at the bedding, pulling it into long, puckered lines. And the top of his head showed, burrowed against the cot—just a glimpse of it—bowed in attempt at concealment, but not inclined deeply enough. And then, just on the other side of that, though his second hand *didn't* show, more of those puckered wrinkles ran over the edge of the bedding at one place, as though it were down below there somewhere out of sight, but hanging on for dear life.

And when she looked at the floor, out beyond the far side of the cot, she could glimpse the lower part of one leg, extended out behind him in a long, lazy sprawl. The other one didn't show, must have been drawn up closer under his body.

"Get up," she sneered. "At least I thought I hated a man. Now I don't know what you are." She passed around the foot of the cot, and his back came into view. He didn't move, but every line of his body expressed the arrested impulse to get away.

Her handbag sprang open, and she pulled something out, pitched it at him. "Here's the five dollars you gave me. Remember?" It fell between his shoulder blades, and lay there lengthwise across his spine, caught in the sharp up-curve his back made, oddly like a label or tag loosely pasted across him.

"You love money so," she said scathingly. "Now here's the interest. Turn around and get it."

She'd fired before she'd known she was going to. As though there were some cue in the words for the gun to take of its own accord, without waiting for her. The crash surprised her; she could feel it go up her whole arm, as though someone had stingingly slapped her wristbone, and the fiery spittle that gleamed for a moment at the muzzle made her blink her eyes and swerve her head aside involuntarily.

He didn't move. Even the five-dollar bill didn't flutter off him. There was a curious low moaning sound from the tubular rod forming the head of the cot, as when a vibration is slowly dimming, and there was a black pockmark in the plaster of the wall, sharply off to one side of it, that seemed to leap up into being for the first time only as her eyes discovered it.

Her hand was at his shoulder now, while her mind was trying to say, "I didn't—I didn't—" He turned over lazily, and ebbed down to the floor, in a way that was almost playful, as if she had been threatening to tickle him and he was trying to avoid it.

Indolent dalliance, his attitude seemed to express. There was even a sort of gashed grin across his mouth.

His eyes seemed to be fixed on her, watching her, with that same detached mockery they'd always shown toward her. As if to say, "What are you going to do now?"

You could hardly tell anything was the matter. There was only a little dark streak by the outside corner of one eye, like a patch of patent leather used instead of court plaster; as though he'd hurt himself there and then covered it over. And where that side of his head had come to rest against the lateral thickness of the bedding, there was a peculiar sworled stain, its outer layers of a lighter discoloration than its core.

Somebody screamed in the confined little room. Not shrilly, but with a guttural wrench, almost like the bark of a terrified dog. It must have been she, for there was no one in there to scream but her. Her vocal cords hurt, as though they had been strained asunder.

"Oh God!" she sobbed in an undertone. "I didn't need to come—"

She cowered away from him, step by faltering step. It wasn't that little glistening streak, that daub of tar, nor yet the way he lay there, relaxed and languid, as if they had had such fun he was exhausted, and it was too much trouble to get up off his back and see her out. It was his eyes that knifed her with fear, over and over, until panic had welled up in her, as though gushing through a sieve. The way they seemed fixed on her, the way they seemed to follow her backward, step by step. She went over a little to one side, and that didn't get her away from them. She went over a little to the other, and that didn't get her away from them either. Contemptuous, patronizing, mocking, to the end; with no real tenderness in them for her, ever. He looked on her in death as he'd looked on her in life.

She could almost hear the drawled words that went with that look. "Where d'you think you're going now? What's your hurry? Come back here, you!"

Her mind screamed back, "Away from here! Out of here! Before somebody comes! Before anybody sees me!"

She turned and fled through the opening, and beat her way through the outside room, flailing with her arms, as though it were an endless treadmill going the other way, trying to carry her back in to him, instead of a space of a brief few yards.

She got to the door and collided against it. But then, after the first impact, after her body was stopped against it, instead of stilling, it kept on thumping, and kept on thumping, as though there were dozens of her hurling themselves against it in an endless succession.

Wood shouldn't knock so, wood shouldn't bang so— Her hands flew up to her ears and clutched them. She was going mad.

The blows didn't space themselves and wait between. They were aggressive, demanding, continuous. They were already angered, and they were feeding on their own anger with every second's added delay. They drowned out, in her own ears, her second, smothered scream of anguish. A scream that held more real fear in it than even the first one had, in the other room just now. Fear, not of the supernatural now, but of the personal, a fear more immediate, a fear more strong. Agonizing fear, trapped fear such as she'd never known existed before. *The fear of losing the thing you love.* The greatest fear there is.

For the voice that riddled the door, that welled through, bated but flinty with stern impatience, was Bill's.

Her heart knew it before the sound came, and then her ears knew it right as it came, and then its words told her after they had come.

"Patrice! Open. Open this door. Patrice! Do you hear me? I knew I'd find you here. Open this door and let me in, or I'll break it down!"

A moment too late she thought of the lock, and just a moment in time he thought of it too. That it had been unlocked the whole while, just as she had found it to be earlier. She crushed herself flat against it, with a whimper of despair, just too late, just as the knob gave its turn and the door seam started to widen.

"No!" she ordered breathlessly. "No!" She tried to hold it closed with the full weight of her whole palpitating body.

She could almost feel the currents of his straining breath beating into her face. "Patrice, you've—got—to—let—me—in—there!"

And between each word she lost ground, her heels scraped futilely backward over the surface of the floor.

He could see her now, and she could see him, through the fluctuating gap their opposing pressures made, widening a little, then narrowing again, then widening more than ever. His eyes, so close to her own, were a terrible accusation, far worse than that dead man's had been inside. Don't look at me, don't look at me! she implored them despairingly in her mind. Oh, turn away from me, for I can't bear you!

Back she went, steadily and irresistibly, and still she tried to bar him, to the last, after his arm was in and his shoulder, straining her whole body insensately against him, flattening her hands till they showed bloodless against the door.

Then he gave one final heave to end the unequal contest, and she was swept back along the whole curved arc of the door's path, like a leaf or a piece of limp rag that got caught in the way. And he was in, and he was standing there next to her, his chest rising and falling a little with quickened breath.

"No, Bill, no!" she kept pleading mechanically, even after the cause of her plea was lost. "Don't come in. Not if you love me. Stay out."

"What're you doing here?" he said tersely. "What brought you?"

"I want you to love me," was all she could whimper, like a distracted child. "Don't come in. I want you to love me."

He took her suddenly and shook her fiercely by the shoulder for a moment. "I saw you. What did you come here to do? What did you come here for, at this hour?" He released her again. "What's this?" He picked up the gun, which she had completely lost track of until now in her turmoil. It must have fallen, or she must have flung it to the floor, in her flight from the inner room.

"Did you bring it with you?" He came back toward her again. "Patrice, *answer* me!" he said with a flinty ferocity she hadn't known he possessed. "What did you come here for?"

Her voice kept backing and filling in her throat, as if unable to rise to the top. At last it overflowed. "To—to—to kill him." She toppled soddenly against him, and his arm had to go around her, tight and firm, to keep her up.

Her hands tried to crawl up his lapels, up his shirtfront, toward his face, like wriggling white beggars pleading for alms.

A swipe of his hand and they were down again.

"And did you?"

"Somebody—did. Somebody—has already. In there. He's dead." She shuddered and hid her face against him. There is a point beyond which you can't be alone anymore. You have to have someone to cling to. You have to have someone to hold you, even if he is to reject you again in a moment or two and you know it.

Suddenly his arm dropped, and he'd left her. It was terrible to be alone, even just for that minute. She wondered how she'd stood it all these months, all these years.

Life was such a crazy thing, life was such a freak. A man was dead. A love was blasted into nothingness. But a cigarette still sent up smoke in a dish. And an ice cube still hovered unmelted in a highball glass. The things you wanted to last, they didn't; the things it didn't matter about, they hung on forever.

Then he reappeared from the other room, stood in the opening looking at her again. Looking at her in such a funny way. A little too long, a little too silent—she couldn't quite make out what it was she didn't like about it, but she didn't like him to look at her that way. Others, it didn't matter. But not him.

Then he raised the gun, which he was still holding, and put it near his nose.

She saw his head give a grim nod.

"No. No. I didn't. Oh, please believe me—"

"It's just been fired," he said quietly.

There was something rueful about the expression of his eyes now, as if they were trying to say to her, Why don't you want to tell me? Why don't you get it out of the way by telling me, and then I'll understand. He didn't say that, but his eyes seemed to.

"No, I didn't. I fired it at him, but I didn't hit him."

"All right," he said quietly, with just that trace of weariness you show when you don't believe a thing, but try to gloss it over to spare someone.

Suddenly he'd thrust it into the side pocket of his coat, as though it were no longer important, as though it were a past detail, as though there were things of far greater moment to be attended to now. He buttoned his coat determinedly, strode back to her; his movements had a sort of lithe intensity to them now that they'd lacked before.

An impetus, a drive.

He swept a sheltering arm around her again. (That sanctuary that she'd been trying to find all her life long. And only had now, too late.) But this time in hurried propulsion toward the door, and not just in support. "Get out of here, quick," he ordered grimly. "Get down to the street again fast as you can."

He was pulling her along, hurrying her with him, within the curve of his protective arm. "Come on. You can't be found here. You must have been out of your mind to come here like this!"

"I was," she sobbed. "I am."

She was struggling against him a little now, trying to keep herself from the door. She pried herself away from him suddenly, and stood back, facing him. Her hands kept rebuffing his arms each time they tried to reclaim her.

"No, wait. There's something you've got to hear first. Something you've got to know. I tried to keep you out, but now you're in here with me. I've come this far; I won't go any further." And then she added, "The way I was."

He reached out and shook her violently, in his exasperation. As if to get some sense into her. "Not now! Can't you understand? There's a man dead in the next room. Don't you know what it means if you're found here? Any minute somebody's apt to stick his head into this place—"

"Oh, you fool," she cried out to him piteously. "You're the one who doesn't understand. The damage has been done already. Can't *you* see that? I *have* been found here!" And she murmured half audibly, "By the only one who matters to me. What's there to run away and hide from now?" She brushed the back of her hand wearily across her eyes. "Let them come. Bring them on now."

"If you won't think of yourself," he urged her savagely, "think of Mother. I thought you loved her, I thought she meant something to you. Don't you know what a thing like this will do to her? What are you trying to do, kill her?"

"Somebody used that argument before," she told him vaguely. "I can't remember who it was or where it was."

He'd opened the door cautiously and looked out. Narrowed it again, came back to her. "No sign of anyone. I can't understand how that shot wasn't heard. I don't think these adjoining rooms are occupied."

She wouldn't budge. "No, this is the time, and this is the place. I've waited too long to tell you. I won't go a step further. I won't cross that doorsill—"

He clenched his jaw. "I'll pick you up and carry you out of here bodily if I have to! Are you going to listen to me? Are you going to come to your senses?"

"Bill, I'm not entitled to your protection. I'm not—"

His hand suddenly clamped itself to her mouth, sealing it. He heaved her clear of the floor, held her cradled in his arms. Her eyes strained upward at him in muted helplessness, above his restraining hand.

Then they dropped closed. She didn't struggle against him.

He carried her that way out the door, and along the hall, and down those stairs she'd climbed so differently a little while ago. Just within the street entrance he set her down upon her feet again.

"Stand here a minute, while I look out." He could tell by her passiveness now that her recalcitrance had ended.

He withdrew his head. "No one out there. You left the car around the corner, didn't you?" She didn't have time to wonder how he knew that. "Walk along close to me. I'm going to take you back to it."

She took his arm within a double coil of her own two, and clinging to him like that, they came out unobtrusively and hurried along together close in beside the building front, where the shadow was deepest.

It seemed a long distance. No one saw them; better still, no one was there to see them. Once, a cat scurried out of a basement vent up ahead of them. She crushed herself tighter against him for a moment, but no sound escaped her. They went on, after the brief recoil.

They rounded the corner, and the car was there, only its own length back away from the corner.

They crossed on a swift diagonal to it, and he unlatched the door for her and armed her in. Then suddenly the door was closed again, between them, and he'd stayed on the outside.

"Here are the keys. Now take it home and—"

"No," she whispered fiercely. "No! Not without you! Where are you going? What are you going to do?"

"Don't you understand? I'm trying to keep you out of it. I'm going back up there again. I have to. To make sure there's nothing there linking you. You've got to help me. Patrice, what was he doing to you? I don't want to know why, there isn't time for that now, I only want to know *what*."

"Money," she said laconically.

She saw his clenched hand tighten on the rim of the door, until it seemed to be trying to cave it in. "How'd you give it to him, cash or check?"

"A check," she said fearfully. "Only once, about a month ago."

He was speaking more tautly now. "You destroyed it when it came back, of c—?"

"I never got it back. He purposely kept it out. He must still have it someplace."

She could tell by the way he stiffened and slowly breathed in, he was more frightened by that than he had been by anything else she had told him so far. "My God," he said batedly. "I've got to get that back, if it takes all night." He lowered his head again, leaned it in toward her. "What else? Any letters?"

"None. I never wrote him a line in my life. There's a five-dollar bill lying in there, by him, but I don't want it."

"I'd better pick it up anyway. Nothing else? You're sure? Now, think, Patrice. Think hard."

"Wait; that night at the dance—he seemed to have my telephone number. Ours. Jotted down in a little black notebook he carries around with him." She hesitated. "And one other thing."

"What? Don't be afraid; tell me. What?"

"Bill—he made me marry him tonight. Out at Hastings."

This time he brought his hand up, let it pound back on the door rim like a mallet. "I'm glad he's—" he said balefully. He didn't finish it. "Did you sign your own name?"

"The family's. I had to. That was the whole purpose of it. The justice is mailing the certificate in to him, here at this address, in a day or two."

"There's still time enough to take care of that, then. I can drive out tomorrow and scotch it out there, at that end. Money works wonders."

Suddenly he seemed to have made up his mind what he intended doing. "Go home, Patrice," he ordered. "Go back to the house, Patrice."

She clung fearfully to his arm. "No— What are you going to do?"

"I'm going back up there. I have to."

She tried to hold him back. "No! Bill, no! Someone may come along. They'll find *you* there. Bill," she pleaded, "for *me*—don't go back up there again."

"Don't you understand, Patrice? Your name has to stay out of it. There's a man lying dead upstairs in that room. They mustn't find anything linking you to him. You never knew him, you never saw him. I have to get hold of those things—that check, that notebook. I have to get rid of them. Better still, if I could only move him out of there, leave him somewhere else, at a distance from here, he mightn't be identified so readily. He might never be identified at all. He's not from town here; there isn't anybody likely to inquire in case of his sudden disappearance. He came and he went again, bird of passage. If he's found in the room there, it'll be at once established who he is, and then that'll bring out a lot of other things."

She saw him glance speculatively along the length of the car, as if measuring its possibilities as a casket.

"I'll help you, Bill," she said with sudden decision. "I'll help you—do whatever you want to do." And then, as he looked at her dubiously, "Let me, Bill. Let me. It's a small way of—making amends for being the cause of the whole problem."

"All right," he said. "I can't do it without the car, anyway. I need that." He crowded in beside her. "Give me the wheel a minute. I'll show you what I want you to do."

He drove the car only a yard or two forward, stopped it again. It now stood so that only the hood projected beyond the corner building line; the rest of it still remained sheltered behind that. The driver's seat was exactly aligned with the row of storefronts around the turn.

"Look down that way, from where you sit," he instructed her. "Can you see that particular doorway from here?"

"No. I can see about where it is, though."

"That's what I mean. I'll stand in it, light up a cigarette. When you see that, bring the car on around in front of it. Until then, stay back here where you are. If you see anything else, if you see something go wrong, don't stay here. Drive straight out and away, without making the turn. Drive for home."

"No," she thought stubbornly, "no, I won't. I won't run off and leave you here." But she didn't tell him so.

He'd gotten out again, was standing there facing her, looking cautiously around on all sides of them, without turning his head too much, just holding his body still, glancing over his shoulders, first on this side, then on that.

"All right," he said finally. "It's all right now. I guess I can go now."

He touched the back of her hand consolingly for a minute.

"Don't be frightened, Patrice. Maybe we'll be lucky, at that. We're such novices at anything like this."

"Maybe we'll be lucky," she echoed, abysmally frightened.

She watched him turn and walk away from the car.

He walked as he always walked; that was one nice thing about him. He didn't slink or cringe. She wondered why that should have mattered to her at such a time as this. But it made what he, what they, were about to attempt to do a little less horrible, somehow.

He'd turned, and he'd gone inside the building where the man was lying dead.

IT SEEMED like an eternity that he'd been up there. She'd never known time could be so long.

That cat came back again, the one that had frightened her before, and she watched its slow, cautious circuitous return to the place from which they had routed it. She could see it while it was still out in the roadway, but then as it closed in toward the building line, the deeper shading swallowed it.

You can kill a rat, she found herself addressing it enviously in her mind, and they praise you for it. And your kind of rat only bites, they don't suck blood.

Something glinted there, then was gone again.

It was surprising how clearly she could see the match flame.

She hadn't expected to be able to. It was small, but extremely vivid for a moment. Like a luminous yellow butterfly held pinned for a second at full wingspread against a black velvet backdrop, then allowed to escape again.

She promptly bore down on the starter, trundled around the corner, and brought the car down to him with facile stealth. No more than a soft whirr and sibilance of its tires.

He'd turned and gone in again before she'd reached him. The cigarette that he'd used to attract her lay there already cast down.

She didn't know where he wanted to—wanted to put what he was bringing out. Front or back. She reached out and opened the rear door on his side, left it that way, ready and waiting for him.

Then she stared straight ahead through the windshield, with a curious sort of rigidity, as though she were unable to move her neck.

She heard the building door open, and still couldn't turn her neck. She strained, tugged at it, but it was locked in some sort of rigor of mortal terror, wouldn't carry her head around that way.

She heard a slow, weighted tread on the gritty sidewalk—his— and accompanying it a softer sound, a sort of scrape, as when two shoes are turned over on their softer topsides, or simply on their sides, and trail along that way, without full weight to press them down.

Suddenly his voice breathed urgently (almost in her ear, it seemed), "The front door. The front."

She couldn't turn her head. But she could move her arms at least. She extended them without looking, broke the latch open for him. She could hear her own breath singing in her throat, like the sound a teakettle spout makes when it is simmering toward a catastrophic overflow.

Someone settled on the seat beside her. Just the way anyone does, with the same crunchy strain on the leather. He touched her side; he nudged her here and there.

The muscular block shattered, and her head swung around.

She was looking into his face. Not Bill's, not Bill's. The mocking eyes wide open in the dark. *His* head had had to swing toward her, just as hers had toward him—it couldn't have remained inert!—to make the grisly face-to-face confrontation complete. Even in death he wouldn't let her alone.

A strangled scream wrenched at her windpipe.

"Now, none of that," the voice of Bill said, from just on the other side of him. "Get in back. I want the wheel. I want him next to me."

The sound of his voice had a steadying effect on her. "I didn't mean it," she murmured blurredly. She got out, got in again, holding on to the car for support in the brief transit between the two places. She didn't know how she did it, but she did.

He must have known what she was going through, though he didn't look at her.

"I told you to go home," he reminded her quietly.

"I'm all right," she said. "I'm all right. Go ahead." It came out tinny, like something on a worn-out disk played by a feathered needle.

The door cracked shut, and they were in motion.

Bill kept the car down to a laggard crawl the first few moments, using only one hand to the wheel. She saw him reach over with the other and tilt down the hat brim low over the face beside him.

He found time for a word of encouragement to her, conscious of her there behind him, though still he didn't turn to glance at her.

"Can you hear me?"

"Yes."

"Try not to be frightened. Try not to think of it. We've been lucky so far. The check and the notebook were on him. Either we make it or we don't. Look at it that way. It's the only way. You're helping me too that way. See, if you're too tense, then I'm too tense too. You react on me."

"I'm all right," she said with that same mechanical bleat as before. "I'll be quiet. I'll be controlled. Go ahead."

After that, they didn't talk. How could you, on such a ride?

She kept her eyes away. She'd look out the side as long as she could; then when that became a strain, she'd look up at the car ceiling for a moment to rest. Or down at the floor directly before her. Anywhere but straight ahead, to where those two heads (she knew) must be lightly quivering in synchronization to the same vibration.

She tried to do what he'd told her. She tried not to think of it. "We're coming home from a dance," she said to herself. "He's bringing me home from the Country Club, that's all. I'm wearing that black net with the gold disks. Look, see? I'm wearing that black dress with the gold disks. We had words, so I'm—I'm sitting in the back, and he's sitting alone up front."

Her forehead was a little cold and damp. She wiped it off.

"He's bringing me home from the movies," she said to herself. "We saw—we saw—we saw—" Another of those blocks, this time of the imagination, occurred; it wouldn't come. "We saw—we saw—we saw—"

Suddenly she'd said to him aloud, "What was the name of that picture we just now came away from?"

"Good," he answered instantly. "That's it. That's a good idea.

I'll give you one. Keep going over it." It took him a moment to get one himself. "Mark Stevens in *I Wonder Who's Kissing Her Now*," he said suddenly. They'd seen that together back in the sunlight, a thousand years ago (last Thursday). "Start in at the beginning and run through it. If you get stuck, I'll help you out."

She was breathing laboredly, and her forehead kept getting damp again all the time. "He wrote songs," she said to herself, "and he took his foster sister to a—to a variety-show, and he heard one of them sung from the stage—"

The car made a turn, and the two heads up front swung together, one almost landed on the other's shoulder. Somebody pried them apart.

She hurriedly squeezed her eyes shut. "When—when did the title song come into it?" she faltered. "Was that the opening number, they heard from the gallery?"

He'd halted for a light, and a taxicab had halted beside him, wheel cap to wheel cap. "No, that was—" He looked at the taxicab. "That was—" He looked at the taxicab again, the way you look vaguely at some external object when you're trying to remember something that has nothing to do with it. "That was 'Hello, Ma Baby.' Cakewalk number, don't you remember? The title song didn't come until the end. He couldn't get words for it, don't you remember?"

The light had changed. The taxicab had slipped on ahead, quicker to resume motion. She crushed the back of her hand against her mouth, sank her teeth into it. "I can't," she sighed to herself. "I can't." She wanted to scream to him, "Oh, open the door! Let me out! I'm not brave! I thought I could, but I can't— I don't care, only let me get out of here, now, right where we are!"

Panic, they called this panic.

She bit deeper into her own skin, and the hot frenzied gush subsided.

He was going a little faster now. But not too fast, not fast enough to attract suspicion or catch any roving eye. They were in the outskirts now, running along the turnpike that breasted the sunken railroad right-of-way. You were supposed to go a little faster along there.

It took her several moments to realize that the chief hazard was over. That they were already out of Caulfield, clear of it, or at least clear of its built-up heart. Nothing had happened. No untoward event. They hadn't grazed any other car. No policeman had come near them, to question them over some infraction, to look into the car. All those things that she had dreaded so had failed to materialize. It had been a ride completely without incident. The two of them might have been alone in the car, for all the risk they'd run—outwardly. But inwardly—

She felt all shriveled up inside, and old, as though there were permanent wrinkles on her heart.

"He wasn't the only one that died tonight," she thought. "I died too somewhere along the way, in this car. So it didn't work; it was all for nothing. Better to have stayed back there, still alive, and taken the blame and the punishment."

They were out in open country now. The last cardboard-box factory, kept at a civic-minded distance away from the city limits, the last disused-brewery stack, even those had long slipped by. The embankment that carried the turnpike had started a very gradual rise, the broad swath of railroad tracks, by illusory contrast, seemed to depress still further. The neat, clean-cut concrete facing that had been given the embankment further in toward town didn't extend this far out; here there was just a natural slope, extremely steep, but with weeds and bushes clinging to it.

He'd stopped all of a sudden, for no apparent reason. Run the two outside wheels off the road on the railroad's side, and stopped there. That was all the space that was allowed, just two wheels of the car; even that was an extremely precarious position to take. The downslope began almost outside the car door.

"Why here?" she whispered.

He pointed. "Listen. Hear it?" It was a sound like the cracking of nuts. Like a vast layer of nuts, all rolling around and being cracked and shelled.

"I'd like to get him out of town," he said. He got out, and scrambled down the slope a way, until she could only see him from the waist up, and stood looking down. Then he picked up something—a stone, maybe, or something—and she saw him throw. Then he turned his head a little and seemed to be listening.

Finally he fought his way back up to her again, digging his feet in sideways to gain leverage.

"It's a slow freight," he said. "Outbound. It's on the inside track, I mean the one right under us here. I could see a lantern go by on the roof of one of the cars. It's unearthly long—I think they're empties—and it's going very slow, almost at a crawl. I threw a stone, and I heard it hit one of the roofs."

She had already guessed, and could feel her skin crawling.

He was bending over the form on the front seat, going through its pockets. He ripped something out of the inside coat pocket. A label or something.

"They don't always get right-of-way like the fast passengers do.

It may have to stop for that big turnpike crossing not far up. You know the one I mean. The locomotive must be just about reaching it by now—"

She'd fought down her repulsion; she'd made up her mind once more, though this was going to be even worse than back there at the doorway. "Shall I— Do you want me to—?" And she got ready to get out with him.

"No," he said, "no. Just stay in it and watch the road. The slope is so steep that when you get down below a certain point with— anything—it will plunge down the rest of the way by itself. It's been sheared off at the bottom, it's a sheer drop."

He'd swung the front door out as far as it would go now.

"How's the road?" he asked.

She looked back first, all along it. Then forward. The way it rose ahead made it even easier to sight along.

"Empty," she said. "There's not a moving light on it anywhere."

He dipped down, did something with his arm, and then the two heads and the two pairs of shoulders rose together. A minute later the front seat was empty.

She turned away and looked at the road, looked at the road for all she was worth.

"I'll never be able to sit on the front seat of this car again," it occurred to her. "They'll wonder why, but I'll always balk, I'll always think of what was there tonight."

He had a hard time getting him down the slope; he had to be a brake on the two of them at once, and the weight was double. Once the two of them went down momentarily, in a stumble, and her heart shot up into her throat, as though there were a pulley, a counterweight, working between them and it.

Then he regained his balance again.

Then when she could only see him from the waist up, he bent over, as if laying something down before him, and when he'd straightened up again, he was alone; she could only see him by himself.

Then he just stood there waiting.

It was a gamble, a wild guess. A last car, a caboose, could have suddenly come along, and—no more train to carry their freight away. Just trackbed left below, to reveal what lay on it as soon as it got light.

But he'd guessed right. The sound of cracking nuts thinned, began to die out. A sort of rippling wooden shudder, starting way up ahead, ran past them and to the rear. Then a second one. Then silence.

He dipped again.

Her hands flew up to her ears, but she was too late. The sound beat her to it.

It was a sick, hollow thud. Like when a heavy sack is dropped. Only, a sack bursts from such a drop. This didn't.

She put her head down low over her lap and held her hands pressed to her eyes.

When she looked up again, he was standing there beside her. He looked like a man who has himself in hand, but isn't sure that he isn't going to be sick before long.

"Stayed on," he said. "Caught on that catwalk, or whatever it is, that runs down the middle of each roof. I could see him even in the dark. But his hat didn't. That came off and went over."

She wanted to scream, "Don't! Don't *tell* me! Let me not know! I know too much already!" But she didn't. And by that time it was over with, anyway.

He got in again and took the wheel, without waiting for the

train to recommence its run. "It'll go on again," he said. "It has to. It was already on its way once. It won't just stand there the rest of the night."

He ran the car back onto the rim of the road again, and then he brought it around in a U-turn, facing back to Caulfield. And still nothing came along, nothing passed them. On no other night could this road have been so empty.

He let their headlight beams shoot out ahead of them now.

"Do you want to come up here and sit with me?" he asked her quietly.

"No!" she said in a choked voice. "I couldn't! Not on *that* seat."

He seemed to understand. "I just didn't want you to be all alone," he said compassionately.

"I'll be all alone from now on, anyway, no matter where I sit," she murmured. "And so will you. We'll both be all alone, even together."

SHE heard the brakes go on and felt the motion of the car stop. He got out and got into the back next to her. They stayed just the way they were for several long moments. She with her face pressed against the bosom of his shirt, buried against him as if trying to hide it from the night and all that had happened in the night. He with one hand to the back of her head, holding it there, supporting it.

They didn't move nor speak at first.

Now I have to tell him, she kept thinking with dread. Now the time is here. And how shall I be able to?

She raised her head at last and opened her eyes. He'd stopped around the corner from their own house. (*His* own. How could it ever be hers again? How could she ever go in there, after what had happened tonight?) He'd stopped around the corner, out of sight of it, and not right at the door. He was giving her the chance to tell him; that must be why he had done it.

He took out a cigarette, and lit it for her in his mouth, and offered it to her inquiringly. She shook her head. So then he threw it out the side of the car.

His mouth was so close to hers; she could smell the aroma of the tobacco freshly on his breath. It'll never be this close again, she thought, never; not after I'm done with what I have to tell him now.

"Bill," she whispered.

It was too weak, too pleading. That feeble a voice would never carry her through. And it had such rocky words ahead of it.

"Yes, Patrice?" he answered quietly.

"Don't call me that." She turned toward him with desperate urgency, forcing her voice to be steady. "Bill, there's something you've got to know. I don't know where to begin it. I don't know how— But, oh, you've got to listen, if you've never listened to me before!"

"Sh, Patrice," he said soothingly. "Sh, Patrice." As though she were a fretful child. And his hand gently stroked her hair; downward, and then downward again, and still downward.

She moaned, almost as though she were in pain. "No—don't—don't—don't."

"I know," he said almost absently. "I know what you're trying so hard, so brokenheartedly, to tell me. That you're not Patrice. That you're not Hugh's wife. Isn't that it?"

She sought his eyes, and he was gazing into the distance, through the windshield and out ahead of the car. There was something almost abstract about his look.

"I know that already. I've always known it. I think I've known it ever since the first few weeks you got here."

The side of his face came gently to rest against her head, and stayed there, in a sort of implicit caress.

"So you don't have to try so hard, Patrice. Don't break your heart over it. There isn't anything to tell."

She gave an exhausted sob. Shuddered a little with her own frustration. "Even the one last chance to redeem myself, you've taken away from me," she murmured hopelessly. "Even that little."

"You don't have to redeem yourself, Patrice."

"Every time you call me that, it's a lie. I can't go back to that house with you. I can't go in there ever again. It's too late now—two years too late, two years—but at least let me tell it to you. Oh God, let me get it out! Patrice Hazzard was killed on the train, right along with your brother. I was deserted by a man named—"

Again he placed his hand over her mouth, as he had at Georgesson's place. But more gently than he had then.

"I don't want to know," he told her. "I don't want to hear. Can't you understand, Patrice?" Then took his hand away, but now she was silent, for that was the way he wanted her to be. And that was the easier way to be. "*Won't* you understand how I feel?" He glanced about for an instant, this way and that, as if helplessly in search of some means of convincing her. Some means that wasn't there at hand. Then back to her again, to try once more, speaking low and from the heart.

"What difference does it make if there once was another Patrice, another Patrice than you, a girl I never knew, some other place and some other time? Suppose there *were* two? There are a thousand Marys, a thousand Janes; but each man that loves Mary, he loves only his Mary, and for him there are no others in the whole wide world. And that's with me too. A girl named Patrice came into my life one day. And that's the only Patrice there is for me in the world. I don't love the name; I love the girl. What kind of love do you think I have, anyway? That if she got the name from a clergyman, it's on; but if she helped herself to it, it's off?"

"But she *stole* the name, took it away from the dead. And she lay in someone else's arms first, and then came into your house with her child—"

"No, she didn't. No," he contradicted her with tender stubbornness. "You still don't see, you still won't see, because you're not the man who loves you. She couldn't have, because she *wasn't,* until I met her. She only began then, she only starts from then. She only came into existence, as my eyes first took her in, as my love first started in to start. Before then there wasn't any she. My love began her, and when my love ends, she ends with it. She has to, because she *is* my love. Before then, there was a blank. A vacant space. That's the way with any love. It can't go back before itself.

"And it's you I love. The you I made for myself. The you I hold in my arms right now in this car. The you I kiss like this, right now . . . right now . . . and now.

"Not a name on a birth certificate. Not a name on a Paris wedding license. Not a bunch of dead bones taken out of a railroad car and buried somewhere by the tracks.

"The name of my love is Patrice to me. My love doesn't know any other name; my love doesn't want any."

He swept her close to him, this time with such quivering violence that she was almost stunned. And as his lips found hers, between each pledge he told her:

"You are Patrice. You'll always be Patrice. You'll *only* be Patrice. I give you that name. Keep it for me, forever."

They lay that way for a long while; one now, wholly one. Made one by love; made one by blood and violence.

Presently she murmured, "And you knew, and you never—?"

"Not right away, not all in a flash. Life never goes that way. It was a slow thing, gradual. I think I first suspected inside of a week or two after you got here. I don't know when I was first sure. I think that day I bought the fountain pen."

"You must have hated me that day."

"I didn't hate you that day. I hated myself, for stooping to such a trick. (And yet I couldn't have kept from doing it, I couldn't have, no matter how I tried!) And do you know what I got from it? Only fear. Instead of *you* being the frightened one, I was. I was afraid that you'd take fright from it, and that I'd lose you. I knew *I'd* never be the one to expose you; I was too afraid I'd lose you that way. A thousand times I wanted to tell you, 'I know. I know all about it,' and I was afraid you'd take flight and I'd lose you. The secret wasn't heavy on you; it was me it weighted down."

"But in the beginning. How is it you didn't say anything in the very beginning? Surely you didn't condone it from the very start?"

"No; no, I didn't. My first reaction was resentment, enmity; about what you'd expect. But for one thing, I wasn't sure enough. And the lives of too many others were involved. Mainly there was Mother. I couldn't risk doing that to her. Right after she'd lost Hugh. For all I knew it might have killed her. And even just to implant seeds of suspicion, that would have been just as bad, that would have wrecked her happiness. Then too I wanted to see what the object was, the game. I thought if I gave you enough rope— Well, I gave you rope and rope, and there was no game. You were just you. Every day it became a little harder to be on guard against you. Every day it became a little easier to look at you, and think of you, and like you. Then that night of the will—"

"You knew what you did, and yet you let them go ahead and—"

"There was no real danger. Patrice Hazzard was the name they put down in black and white. If it became necessary, it would have been easy enough to break it, or rather restrict it to its literal application, I should say. Prove that you and Patrice Hazzard were not identically one and the same and, therefore, that you were not the one intended. The law isn't like a man in love; the law values names. I pumped our lawyer a little on the q.t., without of course letting on what I had on my mind, and what he told me reassured me. But what that incident did for me once and for all was to show me there was no game, no ulterior motive. I mean, that it wasn't the money that was at the bottom of it. Patrice, the fright and honest aversion I read on your face that night, when I came to your door to tell you about it, couldn't have been faked by the most expert actress in creation. Your face got as white as a sheet, your eyes darted around as though you wanted to run out of the house for dear life then and there. I touched your hand, and it was icy-cold. There is a point at which acting stops, and the heart begins.

"And that gave me the answer. I knew from that night on what it was you really wanted, what it was that had made you do it: safety, security. It was on your face a hundred times a day, once I had the clue. I've seen it over and over. Every time you looked at your baby. Every time you said, 'I'm going up to my room.' The way you said '*my* room.' I've seen it in your eyes even when you were only looking at a pair of curtains on the window, straightening them out, caressing them. I could almost hear you say, 'They're mine, I belong here.' And every time I saw it, it did something to me. I loved you a little more than I had the time before. And I wanted you to have all that rightfully, permanently, beyond the power of anyone or anything to ever take it away from you again—"

He lowered his voice still further, till she could barely hear the message it breathed.

"At my side. As my wife. And I still do. Tonight more than ever, a hundred times more than before. Will you answer me now? Will you tell me if you'll let me?"

His face swam fluidly before her upturned eyes.

"Take me home, Bill," she said brokenly, happily. "Take Patrice home to your house with you, Bill."

43

FOR a moment, as he braked and as she turned her face toward it, her overtired senses received a terrifying impression that it was on fire, that the whole interior was going up in flame. And then as she recoiled against him, she saw that bright as the light coming from it was, brazier-bright against the early-morning pall, it was a steady brightness; it did not quiver. It poured from every window, above and below, and spilled in gradations of intensity across the lawn, and even as far as the frontal walk and the roadway beyond, but it was the static brightness of lighted-up rooms. Rooms lighted up in emergency.

He nudged and pointed wordlessly, and on the rear plate of the car already there, that they had just drawn up behind, stood out the ominous "MD." Spotlighted, menacing, beetling, within the circular focus of their own headlights. Prominent as the skull and crossbones on a bottle label. And just as fear-inspiring.

"Dr. Parker," flashed through her mind.

He flung open the door and jumped down, and she was right behind him.

"And we sat talking back there all this time," she heard him exclaim.

They chased up the flagstone walk, she at his heels, out-distanced by his longer legs. He didn't have time to use his key. By the time he'd got it out and put it to where the keyhole had last been, the keyhole was already back out of reach and Aunt Josie was there instead, frightened in an old flowered bathrobe, face as gray as her hair.

They didn't ask her who it was; there was no need to.

"Ever since happass eleven," she said elliptically. "*He's* been with her from midnight straight on through."

She closed the door after them.

"If you'd only phoned up," she said accusingly. "If you'd only leff word where I could reach you." And then she added, but more to him than to Patrice, "Daybreak. I hope the party was wuth it. It sure must have been a good one. I know one thing, it sure coss more than any party you ever went to in your life. Or ever likely to go to."

Patrice screamed out within herself, wincing: How right you are! It wasn't good, no, it wasn't—but oh, how costly!

Dr. Parker accosted them in the upper hall. There was a nurse there with him. They had thought he'd be in with her.

"Is she asleep?" Patrice breathed, more frightened than reassured at this.

"Ty Winthrop's been in there alone with her for the past half hour. She insisted. And when people are quite ill, you overrule them; but when they're even more ill than that, you don't. I've been checking her pulse and respiration at ten-minute intervals."

"That bad?" she whispered in dismay. She caught the stricken look on Bill's face, and found time to feel parenthetically sorry for him even while she asked it.

"There's no immediate danger," Parker answered. "But I can't make you any promises beyond the next hour or two." And then he looked the two of them square in the eyes and said, "It's a bad one this time. It's the daddy of them all."

It's the last one, Patrice knew then with certainty.

She crumpled for a moment, and a scattered sob or two escaped from her, while he and Bill led her over to a hall chair, there beside the sickroom door, and sat her down.

"Don't do that," the doctor admonished her, with just a trace of detachment—perhaps professional, perhaps personal. "There's no call for it at this stage."

"It's just that I'm so worn-out," she explained blurredly.

She could almost read his answering thought. Then you should have come home a little earlier.

The nurse traced a whiff of ammonia past her nose, eased her hat from her head, smoothed her hair soothingly.

"Is my baby all right?" she asked in a moment, calmer.

It was Aunt Josie who answered that. "I know how to look after him," she said a trifle shortly. Patrice was out of favor right then.

The door opened and Ty Winthrop came out. He was putting away his glasses.

"They back yet?" he started to say. Then he saw them. "She wants to see you."

They both started up at once.

"Not you," he said to Bill, warding him off. "Just Patrice. She wants to see her alone, without anyone else in the room. She repeated that several times."

Parker motioned her to wait. "Let me check her pulse first."

She looked over at Bill while they were standing there waiting, to see how he was taking it. He smiled untroubledly. "I understand," he murmured. "That's her way of seeing *me*. And a good way it is too. Just about the best."

Parker had come out again.

"Not more than a minute or two," he said disapprovingly, with a side look at Winthrop. "And then maybe we'll all get together to see that she gets a little rest."

She went in there. Somebody closed the door after her.

"Patrice, dear," a quiet voice said.

She went over to the bed.

The face was still in shadow, because of the way they'd left the lamp.

"You can raise that a little, dear. I'm not in my coffin yet."

Her eyes looked up at Patrice in the same way they had that first day at the railroad station. They were kind. They smiled around the edges. They hurt a little, they were so *trustful*.

"I didn't dream—" she heard herself saying. "We drove out further than we'd intended to. It was such a beautiful night—"

Two hands were feebly extended for her to clasp.

She dropped suddenly to her knees and smothered them with kisses.

"I love you," she pleaded. "That much is true; oh, that much is true! If I could only make you believe it. My mother. You're my mother."

"You don't have to, dear. I know it already. I love you too, and my love has always known that you do. That's why you're my little girl. Remember that I told you this: *you're my little girl.*"

And then she said, very softly, "I forgive you, dear. I forgive my little girl."

She stroked Patrice's hand consolingly.

"Marry Bill. I give you both my blessing. Here—" She gestured feebly in the direction of her own shoulder. "Under my pillow. I had Ty put something there for you."

Patrice reached under, drew out a long envelope, sealed, unaddressed.

"Keep this," Mother Hazzard said, touching the edge for a moment. "Don't show it to anyone. It's just for you. Do not open until—after I'm not here. It's in case you need it. When you're in greatest need, remember I gave it to you—open it then."

She sighed deeply, as though the effort had tired her unendurably.

"Kiss me. It's late. So very late. I can feel it in every inch of my poor old body. *You* can't feel how late it is, Patrice, but *I* can."

Patrice bent low above her, touched her own lips to hers.

"Good-bye, my daughter," she whispered.

"Good night," Patrice amended.

"Good-bye," she insisted gently. There was a faint, prideful smile on her face, a smile of superior knowledge, as of one who knows herself to be the better informed of the two.

LONELY vigil by the window, until long after it had grown light. Sitting there, staring, waiting, hoping, despairing, dying a little. Seeing the stars go out, and the dawn creep slowly toward her from the east, like an ugly gray pallor. She'd never wanted to see daybreak less, for at least the dark had covered her sorrows like a cloak, but every moment of increasing light diluted it, until it had reached the vanishing point, it was gone, there wasn't any more left.

Motionless as a statue in the blue-tinged window, forehead pressed forward against the glass, making a little white ripple of adhesion across it where it touched. Eyes staring at nothing, for nothing was all there was out there to see.

I've found my love at last, only to lose him; only to throw him away. Why did I find out tonight I loved him? Why did I have to know? Couldn't I have been spared that at least?

The day wasn't just bitter now. The day was ashes, lying all around her, cold and crumbled and consumed. No use for pinks and blues and yellows to try to tint it, like watercolors lightly applied from some celestial palette; no use. It was dead. And she was sitting there beside its bier.

And if there was such a thing as penance, absolution, for mistakes that, once made, can never be wholly undone again, can only be regretted, she should have earned it on that long vigil. But maybe there is none.

Her chances were dead and her hopes were dead, and she couldn't atone any further.

She turned and slowly looked behind her. Her baby was awake, and smiling at her, and for once she had no answering smile ready to give him. She couldn't smile; it would have been too strange a thing to fit upon her mouth.

She turned her face away again, so that she wouldn't have to look at him too long. Because, what good did crying do? Crying to a little baby. Babies cried to their mothers, but mothers shouldn't cry to their babies.

Outside, the man came out on that lawn down there, pulling his garden hose after him. Then when he had it all stretched out, he let it lie, and went back to the other end of it, and turned the spigot. The grass began to sparkle, up where the nozzle lay inert, even before he could return to it and take it up. You couldn't see the water actually coming out, because the nozzle was down too flat against the ground, but you could see a sort of iridescent rippling of the grass right there that told there was something in motion under it.

Then he saw her at her window, and he raised his arm and waved to her, the way he had in the beginning, that first day. Not because she was she, but because his own world was all in order, and it was a beautiful morning, and he wanted to wave to someone to show them how he felt.

She turned her head away. Not to avoid his friendly little salutation, but because there was a knocking at her door. Someone was knocking at her door.

She got up stiffly, and walked over toward it, and opened it.

A lonely, lost old man was standing out there, quietly, unassumingly. Bill's father was standing out there, very wilted, very spent. A stranger, mistaking her for a daughter.

"She just died," he whispered helplessly. "Your mother just died, dear. I didn't know whom to go to, to tell about it—so I came to your door." He seemed unable to do anything but just stand there, limp, baffled.

She stood there without moving either. That was all she was able to do too. That was all the help she could give him.

THE leaves were dying, as she had died. The season was dying. The old life was dying, was dead. They had buried it back there just now.

"How strange," Patrice thought. "To go on, before one can go on to something new, there has to be death first. Always, there has to be a kind of death, of one sort or another, first. Just as there has been with me."

The leaves were brightly dying. The misty black of her veil dimmed their apoplectic spasms of scarlet and orange and ochre, tempered them to a more bearable hue in the fiery sunset, as the funeral limousine coursed at stately speed homeward through the countryside.

She sat between Bill and his father.

"I am the Woman of the Family now," she thought. "The only woman of their house and in their house. That is why I sit between them like this, in place of prominence, and not to the outside."

And though she would not have known how to phrase it, even to herself, her own instincts told her that the country and the society she was a part of were basically matriarchal, that it was the woman who was essentially the focus of each home, the head of each little individual family group. Not brazenly, aggressively so, not on the outside; but within the walls, where the home really was. She had succeeded to this primacy now. The gangling adolescent who had once stood outside a door that wouldn't open.

One she would marry and be his wife. One she would look after in filial devotion, and ease his loneliness and cushion his decline as best she could. There was no treachery, no deceit, in her plans; all that was over with and past.

She held Father Hazzard's hand gently clasped in her own, on the one side. And on the other, her hand curved gracefully up and around the turn of Bill's stalwart arm. To indicate: You are mine. And I am yours.

The limousine had halted. Bill got out and armed her down. Then they both helped his father and, one on each side of him, walked slowly with him up the familiar terraced flagstones to the familiar door.

Bill sounded the knocker, and Aunt Josie's deputy opened the door for them with all the alacrity of the novice. Aunt Josie herself, of course, a titular member of the family, had attended the services with them, was on her way back now in the lesser of the two limousines.

She closed the door in respectful silence, and they were home.

It was she who first saw them, Patrice. They were in the library.

Bill and his father, going on ahead, supporting arm about waist, had passed the open doorway obliviously. She had lingered behind for a moment, to give some muted necessary orders.

"Yes, Mrs. Hazzard," Aunt Josie's deputy said docilely.

Yes, Mrs. Hazzard. That was the first time she had heard it (Aunt Josie always called her "Miss Pat"), but she would have that now all her life, as her due. Her mind rolled it around on its tongue, savoring it. Yes, Mrs. Hazzard. Position. Security. Impregnability. The end of a journey.

Then she moved forward and, passing the doorway, saw them.

They were sitting in there, both facing it. Two men. The very way they held their heads—they were not apologetic, they were not disclaiming enough, for such a time and such a place and such a visit. Their faces, as she met them, did not say, "Whenever you are ready." Their faces said, "*We* are ready for you now. Come in to us."

Fear put out a long finger and touched her heart. She had stopped.

"Who are those two men?" she breathed to the girl who had let her in. "What are they doing in there?"

"Oh, I forgot. They came here about twenty minutes ago, asking to see Mr. Hazzard. I explained about the funeral and suggested maybe they'd better come back later. But they said no, they said they'd wait. I couldn't do anything with them. So I just let them be."

She went on past the opening. "He's in no condition to speak to anyone now. You'll have to go in there and—"

"Oh, not old Mr. Hazzard. It's Mr. Hazzard his son they want."

She knew then. Their faces had already told her, the grim way they had both sized her up that fleeting second or two she had stood in the doorway. People didn't stare at you like that, just ordinary people. Punitive agents did. Those empowered by law to seek out, and identify, and question.

The finger had become a whole icy hand now, twisting and crushing her heart in its grip.

Detectives. Already. So soon, so relentlessly, so fatally soon. And today of all days, on this very day.

The copybooks were right, the texts that said the police were infallible.

She turned and hurried up the stairs, to overtake Bill and his father, nearing the top now, still linked in considerate, toiling ascent.

Bill turned his head inquiringly at sound of her hasty step behind them. Father Hazzard didn't. What was any step to him anymore? The only one he wanted to hear would never sound again.

She made a little sign to Bill behind his father's back. A quick little quirk of the finger to show that this was something to be kept between the two of them alone. Then said, trying to keep her voice casual, "Bill, as soon as you take Father to his room, I want to see you for a minute. Will you come out?"

He came upon her in her own room, in the act of lowering an emptied brandy jigger from her lips. He looked at her curiously.

"What'd you do, get a chill out there?"

"I did," she said. "But not out there. Here. Just now."

"You seem to be shaking."

"I am. Close the door." And when he had, "Is he sleeping?"

"He will be in another minute or two. Aunt Josie's giving him a little more of that sedative the doctor left."

She kneaded her hands together, as though she were trying to break each bone separately. "They're here, Bill. About the other night. They're here already."

He didn't have to ask, he knew what she meant by "the other night." There was only one other night for them, there would always be only one, from now on. As the nights multiplied, it would become "that night," perhaps; that was the only alteration.

"How do you know? Did they tell you?"

"They don't have to. I know." She snatched at his coat lapels, as though she were trying to rip them off him. "What are we going to do?"

"*We* are not going to do anything," he said with meaning. "*I'll* do whatever is to be done about it."

"Who's that?" she shuddered, and crushed herself close to him. Her teeth were almost chattering with nervous tension.

"Who is it?" he asked at full voice.

"Aunt Josie," came through the door.

"Let go of me," he cautioned in an undertone. "All right, Aunt Josie."

She put her head in and said, "Those two men that're down there, they said they can't wait for Mr. Hazzard anymore."

For a moment a little hope wormed its way through her stricken heart.

"They said if he don't come down, they'll have to come up here."

"What do they want? Did they tell you?" he said to Aunt Josie.

"I asked 'em twice, and each time they said the same thing. 'Mr. Hazzard.' What kind of an answer is that? They're bold ones."

"All right," he said curtly. "You've told us."

She closed the door again.

He stood for a while irresolute, his hand curled around the back of his neck. Then straightened with reluctant decision, squared off his shoulders, hitched down his cuffs, and turned to face the door. "Well," he said, "let's get it over with."

She ran to join him. "I'll go with you."

"You won't!" He took her hand and put it off his arm, in rough rejection. "Let's get that straight right now. You're staying up here, and you're staying out of it. Do you hear me? No matter what happens, you're staying out of it."

He'd never spoken to her like that before.

"Are you taking me to be your husband?" he demanded.

"Yes," she murmured. "I've already told you that."

"Then that's an order. The first and the last, I hope, that I'll ever have to give you. Now look, we can't tell two stories about this. We're only telling one: mine. And it's one that you're not supposed to know anything about. So you can't help me; you can only harm me."

She seized his hand and put her lips to it, as a sort of godspeed. "What are you going to tell them?"

"The truth." The look he gave her was a little odd. "What did you expect me to tell them? *I* have nothing to lie about, as far as it involves me alone."

He closed the door, and he went out.

46

As SHE found her hands leading the way down for her, one over the other, along the banister rail, while her feet followed them more slowly, a step behind all the way, she realized how impossible it would have been to follow his injunction, remain immured up there, without knowing, without listening; how futile of him to expect it of her. She couldn't have been involved as she was, she couldn't have been a woman at all, and obeyed him. This wasn't prying; you didn't pry into something that concerned you as closely as this did her. It was your right to know.

Hand over hand down the banister, the rest of her creeping after, body held at a broken crouch. Like a cripple struggling down a staircase.

A quarter of the way down, the murmur became separate voices. Halfway down, the voices became words. She didn't go beyond there.

Their voices weren't raised. There was no blustering or angry contradiction. They were just men talking quietly, politely together. Somehow, it struck more fear into her that way.

They were repeating after him something he must have just now said.

"Then you do know someone named Harry Carter, Mr. Hazzard."

She didn't hear him say anything. As though he considered one affirmation on that point enough.

"Would you care to tell us what relationship—what connection—there is between you and this man Carter?"

He sounded slightly ironical when he answered that. She had never heard him that way toward herself, but she caught a new inflection to his voice and recognized it for irony. "Look, gentlemen, you already know. You must, or why would you be here? You want me to repeat it for you, is that it?"

"What we want is to hear it from you yourself, Mr. Hazzard."

"Very well, then. He is a private detective. As you already know. I selected and hired him. As you already know. And he was being paid a fee; he was being retained, to watch, to keep his eye on, this man Georgesson, whom you're concerned with. As you already know."

"Very well, we do already know, Mr. Hazzard. But what we don't already know, what he couldn't tell us, because he didn't know himself, was what was the nature of your interest in Georgesson, why you were having him watched."

And the other one took up where the first had left off. "Would *you* care to tell us that, Mr. Hazzard? Why were you having him watched? What was your reason for doing that?"

Out on the stairs, her heart seemed to turn over and lie down flat on its face. "My God," went echoing sickly through her mind. "Now I come into it!"

"That's an extremely private matter," he said sturdily.

"I see; you don't care to tell us."

"I didn't say that."

"But still, you'd rather not tell us."

"You're putting words into my mouth."

"Because you don't seem to supply us with any of your own."

"It's essential for you to know this?"

"We wouldn't be here if it weren't, I can assure you. This man of yours, Carter, was the one who reported Georgesson's death to us."

"I see." She heard him take a deep breath. And she took one with him. Two breaths, one and the same fear.

"Georgesson was a gambler," he said.

"We know that."

"A crook, a confidence man, an all-around shady operator."

"We know that."

"Then here's the part you don't. Back about—it must be four years ago—three, anyway—my older brother Hugh was a senior at Dartmouth College. He started down here to spend the Christmas holidays at home, with us. He got as far as New York, and then he never got any further. He never showed up. He wasn't on the train that was to have brought him in the next day. We got a long-distance phone call from him, and he was in trouble. He was practically being held there against his will. He'd gotten into a card game, it seems, the night before with this

Georgesson and a few of his friends—set up, of course—and they'd taken him for I don't know how many thousands, which he didn't have, and they wanted a settlement before they'd let him go. They had him good; it had the makings of a first-class mess in it. Hugh was just a high-spirited kid, used to associating with decent people, gentlemen, not that kind of vermin, and he hadn't known how to handle himself. They'd built him up for it all evening long, liquored him up, thrown a couple of mangy chorus girls at him in the various spots they'd dragged him around to first—well, anyway, because of my mother's health and the family's good name, there could be no question of calling the police into it; it would have been altogether too smelly. So my father went up there in person—I went along with him, incidentally—and squared the thing off for him. At about fifty cents to the dollar, or something like that. Got back the I.O.U.'s they'd extorted from the kid. And brought him home with us.

"That's about all there was to it. Not a very new story; it's happened over and over. But naturally, I wasn't likely to forget this Georgesson in a hurry. Well, when I learned he was down here in Caulfield a few weeks ago, showing his face around, I didn't know if it was a coincidence or not, but I wasn't taking any chances. I got in touch with a detective agency in New York and had them send Carter down here, just to try to find out what he was up to.

"And there you have it. Now does that answer your question? Is that satisfactory?"

They didn't say it was, she noticed. She waited, but she didn't hear them say it was.

"He didn't approach you or your family in any way? He didn't molest you?"

"He didn't come near us."

(Which was technically correct, she agreed wryly; she'd had to go to him each time.)

"You would have heard about it before now if he had," he assured them. "I wouldn't have waited for you to look me up. I would have looked you up."

With catastrophic casualness a non sequitur followed. She suddenly heard one of them ask him, "Do you want to bring along a hat, Mr. Hazzard?"

"It's right outside in the hall," he answered dryly. "I'll pick it up as we go by."

They were coming out of the room. With an infantile whimper that was almost like that of a little girl running away from goblins in the dark, she turned and fled up the stairs again, back to her room.

"No! No! No!" she kept moaning with feverish reiteration.

They were arresting him, they were accusing him, they were taking him with them.

DISTRACTED, she flung herself down on the bench before her dressing table. Her head rolled soddenly about on her shoulders, as though she were drunk. Her hair was displaced, burying one eye.

"No! No!" she kept insisting. "They can't— It isn't fair—"

They wouldn't let him go— They'd never let him go again— He wouldn't come back— He'd never come back to her—

"Oh, for the love of God, help me! I can't take any more of this!"

And then, as in the fairy tales, as in the storybooks of old, where everything always comes out all right, where good is good and bad is bad, and the magic spell is always broken just in time for the happy ending, there it was—right under her eyes—

Lying there, waiting. Only asking to be picked up. A white oblong, a sealed envelope. A letter from the dead.

A voice trapped in it seemed to whisper through the seams to her, faint, far away: "When you're in the most need, and I'm not here, open this. When your need is the greatest, and you're all alone. Good-bye, my daughter; my daughter, good-bye . . ."

I, Grace Parmentier Hazzard, wife of Donald Sedgwick Hazzard, being on my deathbed, and in the presence of my attorney and lifelong counselor Tyrus Winthrop, who will duly notarize my signature to this and bear witness to it if called upon to do so by the legally constituted authorities, hereby make the following statement, of my own free will and volition, and declare it to be the truth:

That at approximately 10:30 P.M. on the evening of 24th September, being alone in the house with just my devoted friend and housekeeper, Josephine Walker, and my grandchild, I received a long-distance telephone call from Hastings, in the neighboring state. That the caller was a certain Harry Carter, known to me as a private investigator and employed by my family and myself as such. That he informed me that just a few moments earlier my beloved daughter-in-law, Patrice, the widow of my late son, Hugh, had been driven against her will to Hastings by a man using the name of Stephen Georgesson, and had there been compelled to enter into a marriage ceremony with him under duress. And that at that time, while he spoke to me, they were on their way back here, to this city, together.

Upon receipt of this information, and having obtained from this Mr. Carter the address of the aforementioned Stephen

Georgesson, I dressed myself, called Josephine Walker to me, and told her I was going out, and would be away for only a short time. She tried to dissuade me, and to prevail upon me to reveal my purpose and where I was going, but I would not. I instructed her to wait for me close beside the front door, in order to admit me at once upon my return, and under no circumstances, then or at any later time, to reveal to anyone that I had left the house at that time or under those circumstances. I caused her to take an oath upon the Bible and, knowing the nature of her religious beliefs and early upbringing, knew she would not break it afterward no matter what befell.

I removed and carried with me a gun which habitually was kept in a desk in the library of my home, having first inserted into it the cartridges. In order to lessen recognition as much as possible, I put on the heavy veil of mourning which I had worn at the time of the death of my elder son.

I walked a short distance from my own door, entirely alone and unaccompanied, and at the first opportunity engaged a public taxicab. In it I went to the quarters of Stephen Georgesson, to seek him out. I found he had not yet returned when I first arrived, and I therefore waited, sitting in the taxi a short distance from his door, until I saw him return and enter. As soon as he had, I immediately entered in turn, right after him, and was admitted by him. I raised my veil in order to let him see my face, and I could see that he guessed who I was, although he'd never seen me before.

I asked him if it was true that he had just now forced my dead son's wife to enter a marriage pact with him, as had been reported to me.

He readily admitted it, naming the place and time.

Those were the only words that passed between us. Nothing further was said. Nothing further needed to be.

I immediately took out the gun, held it close toward him, and fired it at him as he stood there before me.

I fired it only once. I would have fired it more than once, if necessary, in order to kill him; it was my full intention to kill him. But having waited to see if he would move again, and seeing that he did not, but lay as he had fallen, then and only then I refrained from firing it any more and left the place.

I had myself returned to my own home in the same taxi that had brought me. Within a short time after, I became extremely ill from the excitement and strain I had undergone. And now, knowing that I am dying, and being in full possession of my faculties and with full realization of what I am doing, I wish to make this statement before I pass away and have it, in the case of wrongful accusation of others, should that occur, brought to the attention of those duly constituted to deal with the matter. But only in such case, not otherwise.

> (*Signed*) Grace Parmentier Hazzard
> (*Witnessed and attested*)
> Tyrus Winthrop, Att'y at Law

She reached the downstairs doorway with it too late. The doorway was empty by the time she swayed that far, and clung there, all dazed and disheveled. They'd gone, and he'd gone with them.

She just stood there in the doorway. Empty in an empty doorway.

48

AND then, there he was at last.

He was so very real, so photographically real down there, that paradoxically, she couldn't quite believe she was seeing him. The very herringbone weave of his coat stood out, as if a magnifying glass were being held to the pattern, for her special inspection. The haggardness of his face, the faint trace of shadow where he needed a shave, she could see everything about him so clearly, as if he were much nearer than he was. Fatigue, maybe, did that, by some reverse process of concentration. Or eyes dilated from long straining to see him, so that now they saw him with abnormal clarity.

Anyway, there he was.

He turned, and came in toward the house. And just before he

took the final step that would have carried him too far in under her to be in sight anymore, his eyes went up to the window and he saw her.

"Bill," she said silently through the glass, and her two hands flattened to the pane, as if framing the unheard word into a benediction.

"Patrice," he said silently from down below, and though she didn't hear him, didn't even see his lips move, she knew that was what he said. Just her name. So little, so much.

Suddenly she'd fled from the room as madly as though she'd just been scalded. The upflung curtain settled down again to true, and the backflung door ricocheted back again toward closure, and she was already gone. The baby's wondering head turned after her far too slowly to catch her in her flight.

Then she stopped short again, below the turn of the stairs, and waited for him there, unable to move any further. Stood waiting for him to come to her.

He left his hat, just as though this were any other time he was returning home, and came on up to where she was standing. And somehow her head, as if it were tired of being all alone, went down upon his shoulder and stayed there against his own.

They didn't speak at first. Just stood there pressed together, heads close. There was no message; there was only—being together.

"I'm back, Patrice," was all he said at last.

She shuddered a little and nestled closer. "Bill, now what will they—?"

"Nothing. It's over. It's already through. At least, as far as I'm concerned. That was just for purposes of identification. I had to go with them and look at him, that was all."

"Bill, I opened this. She says—"

She gave it to him. He read it.

"Did you show it to anyone else?"

"No."

"Don't." He tore it once across, and stuffed the remnants into his pocket.

"But suppose—?"

"It's not needed. His gambler friends are already down on the books for it, by this time. They told me they found evidence to indicate that a big card game had taken place up there earlier that night."

"I didn't see any."

He gave her an eloquent look. "They did. By the time they got there."

She widened her eyes a little at him.

"They're willing to let it go at that. So let us let it go at that too, Patrice." He sighed heavily. "I'm all-in. Feel like I've been on my feet for a week straight. I'd like to sleep forever."

"Not forever, Bill, not forever. Because I'll be waiting around, and that would be so long—"

His lips sought the side of her face, and he kissed her with a sort of blind stupefaction.

"Walk me up as far as the door of my room, Patrice. Like to take a look at the youngster, before I turn in."

His arm slipped wearily around her waist.

"*Our* youngster from now on," he added softly.

49

"MR. WILLIAM Hazzard was married yesterday to Mrs. Patrice Hazzard, widow of the late Hugh Hazzard, at a quiet ceremony at St. Bartholomew's Episcopal Church, in this city, performed by the Reverend Francis Allgood. There were no attendants. Following their marriage, Mr. and Mrs. Hazzard left immediately for a honeymoon trip through the Canadian Rockies."—*All Caulfield morning and evening newspapers.*

WHEN the reading of the will had been concluded—that was on a Monday following their return, about a month later—Winthrop asked the two of them to remain behind a moment after the room had been cleared. He went over and closed the door after the others present had left. Then he went to the wall, opened a built-in safe, and took out an envelope. He sat down at his desk.

"Bill and Patrice," he said, "this is meant for you alone."

They exchanged a look.

"It is not part of the estate, so it concerns no one else but the two of you."

"It is from her, of course. It was transcribed on her deathbed, less than an hour before she died."

"But we already—" Bill tried to say.

Winthrop silenced him with upturned hand. "There were two of them. This is the second. Both dictated to me during the hours of that same night, or I should say, early morning. This follows the other. The first she gave you herself that same night, as you know. The other she turned over to me. I was to hold it until today, as I have done. Her instructions to me were: It is for the two of you alike. It is not to be delivered to the one without the other. When delivered, it is not to be opened by the one without the other. And finally, it is only to be delivered in the case of your marriage. If you were not married at this time, as she wanted you to be—and you know she did, very much—then it was to be destroyed by me, unopened. Singly, it is not for either one of you. United in marriage, it is a last gift to the two of you, from her.

"However. You need not read it if you do not want to. You can destroy it unopened. I am under pledge not to reveal what is in it, even though I naturally know, for I took her words down at the bedside, and witnessed and notarized her signature in my capacity as her attorney. You must, therefore, either read it or not read it for yourselves. And if you do read it, then when you have read it, you are to destroy it just the same."

He waited a moment.

"Now, do you want me to deliver it to you, or do you prefer that I destroy it?"

"We want it, of course," Patrice whispered.

"We want it," Bill echoed.

He extended it to them lengthwise. "You kindly place your fingers on this corner. You on this." He withdrew his own fingers, and they were left holding it.

"I hope it brings you the extra added happiness she wanted you both to have. I know that that is why she did it. She asked me to bless you both, for her, as I gave it to you. Which I do now. That concludes my stewardship in the matter."

They waited several hours, until they were alone together in their room that night. Then when he'd finished putting on his robe, and saw that she had donned a silken bridal something over her nightdress, he took it out of his coat pocket and said, "Now. Shall we? You do want to, don't you?"

"Of course. It's from her. We want to read it. I've been counting the minutes all evening long."

"I knew you'd want to. Come on over here. We'll read it together."

He sat down in an easy chair, adjusted the hood of the lamp over one shoulder. She perched beside him on the arm of the chair, slipped an arm about his shoulders.

The sealing-wax wafers crumbled, and the flap shot upright, under his fingers.

In silent intensity, heads close together, they read:

My beloved children:

You are married by now, by the time this reaches you. (For if you are not, it will not reach you; Mr. Winthrop will tell you all about that.) You are happy. I hope I have given you that happiness. I want to give you even a little more. And trust and pray that out of your plenty, you will spare a little of it for me, even though I am gone and no longer there with you. I do not want a shadow to cross your minds every time you recall me. I cannot bear to have you think ill of me.

I did not do that thing, of course. I did not take that young man's life. Perhaps you have already guessed it. Perhaps you both know me well enough to know I could not have done such a thing.

I knew that he was doing something to threaten Patrice's happiness, that was all. That was why we were having Mr. Carter investigate him. But I never actually set eyes on him, I never saw him.

I was alone in the house last night (for as Mr. Winthrop writes this for me, it is still last night, though you will not read it for a long time to come). Even Father, who never goes out without me, had to attend an important emergency meeting at the plant. It meant settling the strike that much sooner, and I pleaded with him to go, though he did not want to. I was alone, just Aunt Josie and the child and I.

Mr. Carter phoned around ten-thirty o'clock and told me he had bad news; that a marriage service had just been performed joining the two of them at Hastings. I had taken the call on the downstairs phone. The shock brought on an attack. Not wishing to alarm Aunt Josie, I tried to get up the stairs to my room unaided. By the time I had reached the top, I became exhausted and could only lie there, unable to move any further or to call out.

While I was lying there helpless like that, I heard the outside door open and recognized Bill's step below. I tried to attract his attention, but my voice was too weak, I couldn't reach him with it. I heard him go into the library, stay there several moments, then come out again. Afterward I remembered hearing something click between his hands right then, as he stood there by the door. And I knew he never uses a cigarette lighter. Then he left the house.

When Aunt Josie had come out some time later, found me there, and carried me to my bed, and while we were waiting for the doctor, I sent her to the library to see if that gun that belonged there was still there. She did not understand why I wanted her to do this, and I did not tell her. But when she came back and told me that the gun was missing, I was afraid what that might mean.

I knew by then that I was dying. One does. I had time to think, lying there during those next long hours. I could think so clearly. I knew that there was a way in which either my Bill or my Patrice might need my protection, once I was no longer there to give it. I knew I had to give it nonetheless, as best I could. I wanted them to have their happiness. I wanted above all my little grandchild to have his security, his start in life without anything to mar it. I knew what the way was in which I could give this to them.

So as soon as Dr. Parker would allow it, I had Ty Winthrop called to my bedside. To him, in privacy, I dictated the sworn statement which you have had by now.

I hope, my dear ones, you have not had to use it. I pray you have not, and never will have to.

But this is its retraction. This is the truth, just meant for you two alone. One tells the truth to one's loved ones, one does not have to swear to and notarize it. There is no guilt upon me. This is my wedding gift to you. To make your happiness even more complete than it is already.

Burn it after you have read it. This is a dying woman's last wish. Bless you both.

Your devoted Mother

The match made a tiny snap. Stripes of black crept up the paper, then ran together, before any flame could be seen. Then there was a little soundless puff, and suddenly yellow light glowed all around it.

And as it burned, over this yellow light, they turned their heads and looked at one another. With a strange, new sort of fright they'd never felt before. As when the world drops away, and there is nothing left underfoot to stand on.

"*She* didn't do it," he whispered, stricken.

"*She* didn't," she breathed, appalled.

"Then—?"

"Then—?"

And each pair of eyes answered, "You."